Danger by Association
The Riverhill Trilogy: Book 3

by

Heather Burnside

Danger by Association

The Riverhill Trilogy: Book 3

by

Heather Burnside

DM Publishing

Also by Heather Burnside:

Slur – The Riverhill Trilogy: Book 1
A Gangster's Grip – The Riverhill Trilogy: Book 2

Crime, Conflict & Consequences – Short Story Collection

***

Introduction

'Danger by Association' is set in Manchester in 1996. As with book 2 of the Riverhill Trilogy, 'Danger by Association' takes place during a period of unrest due to inter-gang rivalry. This period saw high levels of gun crime, gang warfare and drug-related crime in the city. Thankfully, the levels of these types of crime in Manchester have decreased substantially since that time, following a series of measures adopted by the authorities.

Although this book is a work of fiction, it is a gritty crime novel covering the topics described above as well as others. This is therefore reflected in the content, which includes violent scenes and bad language. I apologise if readers find these aspects offensive, but I have included them because I want to give a realistic portrayal.

Part of the novel is based on an actual event. However, I have fictionalised certain parts of that event. Therefore, the characters featured were not involved in the incident, but they are a representation. The name of the hospital and the newspaper are also fictitious.

'Danger by Association' contains a lot of local vernacular. It is usually possible to understand the meanings of words from the context in which they are presented. However, if you want to check out any of the meanings, you can find a good online dictionary of slang words and phrases at: http://www.peevish.co.uk/slang/.

***

Prologue

Iraq 1991

The men were directed to an Iraqi installation with a communications tower. Their job was to destroy the tower and the control buildings surrounding it. John was part of the fire support group. He would provide cover while the demolition teams completed their task.

They carried out a recce beforehand, checking the size and security of the compound. The heat registered by a thermal imager had established that there were bodies inside tents. There was no movement within, indicating that the inhabitants were probably asleep. Acting on this information, the soldiers followed the safest route of entry.

They crept into the compound in the middle of the night; their chosen time of operation when it was easier to remain obscured. The arid, sandy ground was uneven, forming small hillocks, which they used for cover as they made their approach. Despite the heat of day, it was now bitterly cold.

The chill of night, mingled with anticipation, sent a spontaneous shiver through John's body. It was so quiet that he could hear the steady patter of booted feet heading towards the compound, and could almost detect his own thundering heartbeat.

As they sneaked through the entrance to the complex, John felt his adrenalin surge, aware of their proximity to the sleeping Iraqi soldiers. He was surprised how easy it was to enter and wondered why none of the Iraqis had been on guard. Someone would be in the shit after this, he thought sardonically.

Once inside, John's job was to find cover and keep watch.

The tower was in an area at the centre of the compound. The outlying areas were like a tented village, full of sleeping soldiers, vehicles and other equipment.

John and his mate Steve headed for a bank of sandbags, taking care to remain quiet. They secreted themselves behind the bags and took up firing positions. Either side of the wall of sandbags were Iraqi army vehicles: a Land Rover to the right of John, and another to his left, nearer to Steve. The backs of both Land Rovers were aligned with the sandbags. Other members of the fire support group spread out around the compound, keeping themselves concealed.

John faced towards the tower, his night vision picking out distant shadows in the gloom. The group watched for a signal from the demolition team, letting them know the charges were fitted and the timers set. Then they could make their retreat.

John's heart beat in rhythm like the seconds on a clock as they waited in eerie silence. He remained alert; his senses fine-tuned to respond to any sign of danger. He was perspiring in spite of the cold, and could smell a potent mix of spicy food, dust and fear.

Then the silence was broken by a thud coming from the other side of the Land Rover near Steve. It was somebody alighting from the vehicle. Without speaking, they both knew what they needed to do.

Steve crept behind the Land Rover ready to take aim. John moved in closer to the right side of the vehicle. He crouched low behind the sandbags. While taking position he listened for oncoming footsteps. He identified them, moving away from the vehicle and round the front.

Steve moved round the vehicle so he could attack from behind. John anticipated that someone would emerge from in front of the Land Rover at any moment. Unless Steve stopped him. But John was there first.

The Iraqi soldier turned to face John as though sensing a presence. John held off momentarily, wary of breaking the silence. Once Steve reached him, they could take him prisoner. He stared at the Iraqi. A boy, no more than seventeen or eighteen. Their eyes met for an instant. Long enough for John to see the fear on the young boy's face. He knew the boy had spotted him. As the Iraqi aimed his rifle, John beat him to it. He didn't have a choice. He had to take him out at close range.

The sound of gunfire awoke the sleeping Iraqis. They swarmed from their tents, half-dressed but armed, firing a deluge of bullets. Steve raced towards the sandbags while John fired covering shots. But Steve didn't make it. A shot in his right thigh felled him. John had to break cover and drag him back.

They made it to the sandbags. A bullet narrowly missed John, piercing one of the sacks, which spewed a stream of sand onto the dusty terrain.

"Keep firing!" shouted John, and Steve responded. As he gasped in pain from the open leg wound, he carried on shooting at the oncoming Iraqis.

They held their position for several minutes. The enemy were still at a distance, and John was rewarded by the occasional sight of an enemy soldier dropping to the ground. Eventually, three other team members came to join them behind the sandbags.

"Come on, we need to get the fuck out of here!" ordered one.

"Steve's injured," said John, "You'll have to help me get him out while the others cover us."

They headed towards the exit, firing continuous shots to hold the Iraqis off. John and a colleague supported Steve between them, his legs dragging behind and leaving a trail of blood on the ground. John was thankful when they reached their vehicles and broke away from the enemy.

While he was caught up in the firefight, John didn't have time to think about the young boy he had killed. That would follow, in the months after he returned from Iraq. The young boy's terrified face and splattered insides would return to him in sweat-drenched dreams night after torturous night.

Chapter 1

Saturday 8ᵗʰ June 1996

Rita walked in front of her family and greeted them before taking her seat at the front of the church. Her mother, Joan, was seated to her left, resplendent in her new outfit from C & A. To the left of Joan was Rita's father, Ged, looking uncomfortable in his one best suit. As Rita cast her eyes across the front pew she noticed him loosening his shirt collar and adjusting his tie.

Furthest away from Rita, and occupying the inside seat of the pew, was her brother, John, nervously awaiting his bride-to-be, with his best man Tony buoying him up. Rita smiled at John before switching her attention to her husband, Yansis.

Rita felt mixed emotions as she thought about the absent family member. It was five years since her sister, Jenny, had died but on days like today she missed her more than ever. This was the first time Rita had returned to Manchester since Jenny's death. She lived in Greece, where she and Yansis ran a restaurant.

Her sister's demise was such a traumatic event that Rita had taken a lot of persuading before she agreed to return to Manchester. But how could she miss her brother's wedding? So here she was. But only on the condition that she went nowhere near the Riverhill Estate. The place where it had happened. The place where her parents still lived.

Although Rita no longer lived in Manchester, she thought of her sister daily. She always would. Every time she looked at her son's face she was reminded of Jenny. Because, even though Rita and Yansis called Daniel their son, it was Jenny who had given birth to him. As Rita thought about Jenny, she gazed with affection at Daniel who was shuffling impatiently in his seat between her and Yansis.

"It won't be long now till the bride gets here," she whispered as she took in his familiar features and gave his shoulder a gentle squeeze.

As though in response to her words, the organist began to play the wedding march. Rita, along with almost everyone else, turned to see the bride walk up the aisle, which was lined with exquisite blossoms in a delicate pink and white colour scheme.

Rita had never met Paula in person; she had only seen her in photographs. She was a stunning girl, and Rita felt happy for John who gazed proudly at her as she approached. Paula looked radiant in her beautiful off-the-shoulder wedding gown with sweetheart neckline. The onlookers were captivated as she progressed down the aisle, the layers of tulle flowing from a tiny fitted waist against which she clutched a lovely bouquet. Yes, John had definitely done himself proud and, if her parents were to be believed, Paula was a lovely person too.

As the bride drew closer, Rita caught the eye of her best friend, Julie, sitting a few rows back with her husband, Vinny. A few seconds later, the bride joined John at the front of the church, and the wedding march died down. The congregation cleared their throats and hushed their children, and the vicar allowed them time to settle down before beginning the ceremony.

Joan had already broken out her tissues and sat sniffing throughout the entire service. Rita wondered whether it was through happiness for John or sorrow at her missing child. Maybe it was a combination of the two. Rita's mind wandered again to the last time the family had been together, apart from John who had been stationed abroad in the army.

The hospital. The endless wait. Desperately hoping she'd pull through. The devastating news from the doctor. Rita stopped herself, determined not to succumb to tears. This was a happy occasion and she'd make damn sure she enjoyed it. She tried to ignore her mother's whimpering as she focused on the ceremony.

Once outside, the emotional strain was forgotten amidst the excited chatter, words of congratulations and organising the photographs. Rita was too busy to think about emotions as she and Yansis had resolved to keep Daniel clean and tidy at least until the pictures were taken.

Although he was a good child, he was a typical five-year-old boy. Carried away by the novelty and excitement of the occasion, he was more intent on racing around the manicured church lawns than posing for photographs in a stuffy suit.

"Oh, it was lovely wasn't it?" said Julie as she and Vinny joined them on the lawn after the photographs had been taken. "I was filling up when she walked down the aisle in that gorgeous dress."

"Don't be so bleedin' soft, you daft sod," said Rita. "You're supposed to be happy, not crying your eyes out. You're as bad as my mam. I think she went through a full packet of man-sized by the time it was over."

"You're bloody heartless you, Rita," laughed Julie.

They circulated for a while, chatting to friends and relatives until it was time to go to the wedding reception. Then they crowded into a minibus, which John and Paula had laid on especially for the occasion. Within minutes they arrived at the venue, which was a hotel.

It wasn't long before they were all seated ready for the wedding breakfast. But they had to go through the speeches first. This was the moment Rita was dreading. She knew it

7

would be emotional. John was bound to mention Jenny. There was no way he would ignore her absence.

Unlike the church service though, where she had a front row seat, Rita was now surrounded by people on all sides. If she became overcome by emotion it would be difficult to hide. And she didn't want to get upset. This was John and Paula's big day, and despite Jenny no longer being with them, it should nevertheless be a happy one.

After dreading the speeches, she was surprised at how smoothly it went. John handled the matter well and she felt proud of him.

"I want to propose a toast to all our loved ones who sadly can't be with us," he said as he held up his glass. Everybody raised their glasses in respect and John quickly added, "I'm sure they'd want us all to enjoy this day so I don't want to see any tears."

Rita's mother took a deep breath and shoved her tissues inside her handbag.

Daniel was fidgety during the meal and couldn't wait to run around outside with his newfound friends. Fortunately, the wedding reception was in a hotel within its own grounds so he could play out safely. Once he had eaten enough, Rita and Yansis let him go. Then it was time for the adults to relax. While Daniel played outside, Rita and Julie chatted to some of Rita's older relatives. They were all interested in Rita's life in Greece and she enjoyed telling them all about it, as well as discussing her wider family.

When the meal was finished, Rita, Yansis, Julie and Vinny found somewhere else to sit while the hotel staff cleared the tables ready for the evening reception. Yansis and Vinny soon struck up a conversation while the girls chatted amongst themselves.

"That grand aunty of yours was a card, Rita," remarked

Julie. "She could hardly take her eyes off Yansis."

"I know; did you hear what she said?" Rita asked, before answering her own question. "'I've always liked the Mediterranean men myself. They're really sexy.' I had to wedge myself between her and Yansis to protect him. She might be in her seventies but there's life in the old girl yet."

Rita and Julie laughed heartily, and Rita soon felt as though she had been teleported back ten years. To the good times of her younger days. All the great nights out she had spent with Julie and the girls. That was before life got in the way, and a series of traumatic experiences had changed her and Julie irrevocably. But today she was going to be relaxed and carefree.

"There are some right eccentrics in our family, Julie," Rita continued, "The bloody Addams family have got nothing on us."

Then, spotting her Aunty Irene heading towards them, she added, "Talking of which, here's one now, Aunty Irene, my dad's sister, got a tongue on her like a viper."

She whispered the last few words as her Aunty Irene came within earshot.

"Hello Rita, I thought it was you," she announced once she reached them.

"Hello Aunty Irene," sighed Rita.

"Well, aren't you going to introduce me then? I've never met your husband; I wasn't at *your* wedding. Is this him?"

Rita made the introductions, and Yansis, Vinny and Julie shook her aunty's hand politely. Once Aunty Irene had the attention of everyone around the table, she asked Rita, "Was that Jenny's son I saw earlier? Good-looking little lad, isn't he? Takes after his mother."

"No!" said Rita. "You saw Daniel, my son; mine and Yansis's."

Yansis, Julie and Vinny looked on, aware of Rita's feelings about Daniel, as the aunty continued.

"Yes but, you know what I mean."

"As far as Daniel is concerned, me and Yansis are his parents and I don't want anyone telling him anything different."

"But surely he'll have to find out eventually?" Aunty Irene asked. "He'll know there's something amiss; even Yansis isn't as dark as Daniel."

"He'll find out when he's old enough and when we decide to tell him. But that won't be for a long time. He's only five years old, for God's sake! It's too much for him to take in."

Rita could feel her temper rising but she tried to hold it in check. She didn't want to spoil her brother's wedding by having a set to with her Aunty Irene, but her aunty wasn't finished yet.

"Alright, I can see you're upset. I know you don't want to be reminded about Jenny. It was a sad day when she died. Your mother and father were broken-hearted, and when you took that little boy away they were beside themselves …"

"What do you mean?" Rita cut in before she had a chance to carry on.

"Well, you weren't here of course. You'd taken him all the way to Greece, but I was the one having to console them when they were missing him."

"You could have bloody well fooled me!" Rita snapped, unable to put up with her aunty's venom any longer. "My dad couldn't get rid of him quick enough. He was too frightened of him cramping his style. So don't you go telling me they were pining for him! And as for you; we only bloody see you at weddings and funerals."

Her aunty was speechless following this outburst. Rita

was about to continue but, before she could say any more, she felt a tug on her arm.

"Rita, didn't you want to go and talk to John and his new wife?" asked Julie. "There's nobody with them now. Come on while we've got a chance."

Julie's words brought Rita to her senses. She stood up, grabbed her handbag, slammed her chair underneath the table and walked away with Julie. As they were walking off, Rita could hear her aunty shouting after her, "That child should be here with his family; not miles away, living with a load of strangers. What you did was wicked!"

"Did you hear that?" Rita asked Julie, "The cheeky cow!" Rita turned, about to retaliate, but Julie kept a tight grip on her arm.

"Don't rise to it, Rita. Don't let her spoil your brother's wedding. If you go back, you'll be letting her win. Come on!"

For a few moments Rita hovered, indecisive, but Julie's insistent tugging at her arm persuaded her to keep walking. Rita didn't head straight for John and his bride though. She was too annoyed, and needed to calm down first. She and Julie made their way outside the room where they found some ladies' toilets in a different part of the hotel. Rita wanted to vent her anger without being overheard.

Once they were inside, they checked the cubicles. While Julie tapped on each of the doors to make sure they weren't occupied, Rita hammered and kicked at them. It was her way of letting go of her rage at the same time. She had just moved away from one cubicle and was attacking the next one when the door opened. A young woman emerged looking terrified. Without making eye contact, and not even stopping to wash her hands, she swiftly exited the ladies' toilets.

"Bloody hell, Rita; you've frightened the life out of the poor sod!" said Julie.

This realisation caused a break in the tension and Rita stopped kicking at the doors, "I'm sorry, Julie. I didn't mean to go off on one. But thanks for pulling me away; it's a good job you did."

"I know you, Rita. I could see she was annoying you."

Rita fished inside her bag for her cigarettes and lighter while sounding off to Julie, "She's a cheeky cow! What business is it of hers? I wouldn't mind but when I was at home she hardly ever came to see my mam and dad, so what would she know?"

Julie gave her time to let off steam. They knew each other so well that Julie could predict exactly how she would react. After a few minutes of venting, she began to settle down, "Eh, I hope Yansis and Vinny were alright being left with her."

"Don't worry about them two; I'm sure they can handle her. She probably went off with her tail between her legs once you'd given her a piece of your mind."

"I'm not so sure, Julie. She's a nasty old bitch by all accounts." Rita then apologised again, now she was feeling calmer. "I'm sorry Jules, I didn't mean to go off on one."

"It's OK, Rita. It wasn't your fault; I'd have felt the same."

"Look, I'm not gonna let that evil old cow get to me. This is our John's wedding and I'm gonna bloody well enjoy it."

And she meant what she said. Once she had finished her cigarette and calmed herself down, they returned to the reception, passing her dad on the way. She couldn't fail to miss him; he was so loud. But she wasn't going to let that worry her.

She could have become irritable watching him make an arse of himself, boasting loudly about his latest scam, but she wouldn't. She could have focused on her dead sister, but she wouldn't. No, she was going to make the best of things. After all, that was what she had come back to Manchester for: to enjoy her brother's wedding. With that in mind, she and Julie went off to chat to Rita's brother and to introduce themselves properly to Paula.

Chapter 2

Raeni was making the most of some free time while the children were out. It was rare for her to have a bit of peace and quiet. She placed her cup of coffee on a side table and heaved her bulky form into the armchair, her chest wheezing. She didn't bother switching on the TV, but sat there taking a few moments to reflect as she looked around her living room at all her reminders of home. The treasured mementoes she had gathered over time.

Photographs of overseas relatives adorned the walls alongside those of her children. She glanced at a cushion, its cover embroidered with the map of Jamaica. She'd had it longer than she could remember; so long that its colours were now fading and the material was worn away at the seams. A couple of ornamental wedding presents Raeni had brought over in the sixties. Brightly painted bowls and plates that she valued too much for everyday use, and had kept as ornaments instead. Those ornaments had survived for over three decades.

She began to reminisce, thinking of the people she had left behind all those years ago. She thought of her lovely sister, Rose, still over there, and her parents who'd lived out their lives in their homeland. Unfortunately, she hadn't been able to afford the travel to attend their funerals so she could pay her last respects.

On days like today she missed them so much; days when her burden seemed heavier than ever. She'd already lost her eldest son, Leroy, five years ago because of his involvement with gangs, and now her other sons were running wild.

As she sat drinking her coffee, she wondered how it had all gone wrong. Life had looked so promising when Raeni travelled to Britain with Leroy's father in the sixties. He was the one with the work permit, she was the one who was going to raise the children. She trusted him until he left her for another woman, with a young son to feed and no job. She didn't have enough money for the fare home so she had to make the most of a bad situation; alone, just her and her child, in a strange country.

Then, a few years later, she'd met Errol who'd taken an instant dislike to Leroy because he wasn't his son. The poor child bore the brunt of all his disapproval until he was old enough to do something about it.

One night, when Errol dished out too many smacks, Leroy turned on him. His festering resentment spilt over and he reacted aggressively, striking such fear into Errol that he packed his bags and left soon afterwards. Raeni had been on her own ever since, just her and the children.

There was a change in Leroy from that day. Although still only sixteen years of age, he took on the role of family protector. He was constantly trying to prove himself as though he needed to reassure everyone that he was the tough guy, that no one would ever put on him again. Raeni guessed that it must have been around that time that he became involved with gangs. She knew no good would come of it, but was powerless to control him. In the end, she had no choice but to stand by while he followed a path of self-destruction.

And to think, she'd travelled to Britain for a better life. Look where that had landed her. Her remaining two sons were on the wrong side of the law, hanging out with gangs. They were probably dealing in drugs and God knows what else, especially Jamal who was now her eldest. He didn't tell her everything; he knew her feelings on the subjects of gangs and drugs. No matter what lies Jamal told her, she had a good idea what he got up to.

Yes, she knew. Raeni had seen it all before with Leroy. And she worried about it every day. She tried to bring them up right but what chance did she have? There were too many people outside the home who were poisoning their minds. Filling their heads with get-rich stories about drug money.

Her only consolation was that she had given birth to two daughters: Laticia and Corine. At least they weren't running around with gangs, although her youngest, Corine, could be a handful. She was still a teenager, though, and maybe she would grow out of it in time.

Thankfully, Laticia was doing alright since she'd set up home with her boyfriend. He seemed a nice enough lad; pray to God that he treated her right and that she had found some happiness. At times she felt as though Laticia was the only one who kept her sane.

***

Saturday 8th June 1996
Rita had only had a chance for a quick handshake with John and Paula up to this point as they had been surrounded by eager relatives from leaving the church until they arrived at the reception. John was Rita's only remaining sibling. She had always got on well with him and, not having seen him for years, she wanted to make the most of their time together.

"Hiya, John," Rita greeted, giving her brother a hug. Then, turning to Paula, she said, "It's lovely to meet you at long last. I've been dying to meet the woman who's brave enough to take him on."

"Ha ha," said John.

As Rita hugged Paula, John noticed Julie standing at Rita's side.

"Julie, I thought it was you. Bloody hell, it's been a long time."

"It has," said Julie, taking in John's height and broad frame. "I think you were a cheeky teenager last time I saw you."

"Yeah, I was in the forces a long time, but I've been home for a bit now."

"Oh yeah, you're with the police now aren't you? PC Plod, is it, or do you have some other fancy title we have to call you?" teased Rita.

Rita noticed John and Paula exchange a fleeting look before he replied, but she dismissed it as an affectionate glance between two people very much in love.

"John will do," he laughed.

"I like your dress, Paula, and the bridesmaids look gorgeous," commented Julie.

They all soon became engaged in conversation, catching up on the missing years and keeping Paula entertained with anecdotes. When Rita and John began pointing out members of the wider family to Paula and telling her their backstories, Julie made a subtle excuse to slip away.

Rita found that she got along well with Paula who introduced her to several of her relatives. Eventually it became evident that other people were also vying for the bride and groom's attention.

"Listen, I'm gonna get back to Yansis now," said Rita, "But you'll have to try and come over and meet him properly if you get a minute. When do you go on your honeymoon?"

"We're having a deferred one," said John.

"Why?"

"Why do you think?"

"Because we wanted to spend some time with you while you're over here," said Paula.

"You're joking!" Rita was touched. "You shouldn't have delayed your honeymoon on my account."

"It's no problem," said John. "You're only here for a couple of weeks, aren't you?"

"Yes, it's fine," added Paula. "We don't have to go away straightaway so me and John decided that we would stay around till you're back in Greece. You two have got a lot of catching up to do, and I'm looking forward to getting to know you and Yansis. In fact, we'd like you both to come for dinner. You can bring Daniel too if you want."

"Aah, that's really nice of you, thank you. Right, we'll catch you later then, and we can sort out the details."

Rita made her way back to Yansis, Julie and Vinny, stopping en route to chat with her mother. By the time Rita returned, she had calmed down. Because of her resolve to enjoy the wedding and deal with any problems when it was over, Rita put on an act of indifference. Looking at her, nobody would have guessed what was on her mind.

As day turned into evening, more guests arrived. When the room was almost full, the DJ announced that it was time to get the bride and groom on the dance floor. Everybody broke into applause as the DJ played 'How Deep is Your Love' by Take That.

"Bloody hell, Jules. I think we must be getting old. I still remember the original version of this."

"The Bee Gees," they both said together.

"Eh, we're not too old yet, Rita. I'll have you on that dance floor once the music speeds up a bit."

"Depends what it is," she replied.

As the sound of Take That faded, the music to Bobby Brown's 'Two Can Play that Game' filled the room, and the girls were soon on the dance floor. That set the tone for the rest of the evening, and Rita put her troubles aside.

***

Saturday 8th June 1996

They had just arrived back at Julie and Vinny's home, a substantial four-bedroomed Victorian semi-detached in the middle-class suburb of Heaton Moor. The house was in silence as Julie and Vinny's children were staying overnight with their grandparents. Daniel had fallen asleep in the car so they were doing their best not to wake him up while Yansis carried him inside.

"I'll just help Yansis put Daniel to bed, then I'll be back down for a chat," whispered Rita.

Yansis went straight to bed and when Rita came back downstairs without him, Vinny decided to go too.

"I'll leave you two to chat," he said.

"How are you feeling?" Julie asked Rita once they were alone.

"Fine, it was a lovely day."

"Yeah, it was, but how are you *really* feeling Rita? You might put on a brave face to the rest of the world but you can't fool me. I've known you too long."

A tentative smile crossed Rita's lips, then she replied. "Oh, you know. It was never gonna be easy, was it? But it didn't go too bad under the circumstances."

"Are you still annoyed with your aunty?"

"A bit. She's always been a nasty piece of stuff, and I could have done without that on top of everything else."

"Well, like you say, it was never gonna be easy but it's over now."

"It's not just that, Julie."

"What do you mean?"

Rita took a deep breath before continuing. "I didn't get round to telling you but, according to my mam, Raeni's asked about Daniel a lot over the years. She made it clear she wasn't happy about me and Yansis taking him abroad. It seems like, suddenly, every bugger wants a slice of him."

Raeni was Daniel's biological grandmother although she had never seen her grandchild. Her son, Leroy, died before Daniel was born. Rita and Yansis then took on responsibility for Daniel; it was what Jenny requested before she too had passed away.

"Ah, no wonder it struck a chord when your aunty started going on about you taking him," said Julie.

"No, it was after that when my mam told me. But, it's not like I haven't already thought about it in the past. I tell you what though, they can all say what they bleedin' well like, Julie, but I know we did the right thing."

"Of course you did, Rita."

"Dead right! What sort of a life would he have had on the Riverhill? Dealing drugs and hanging about with gangs like his father? I'd already decided to steer clear of the place after what happened to Jenny, but I'm even more determined now. I don't want Leroy's family anywhere near Daniel! I don't trust them one bit; I don't trust anyone who's related to Leroy.

"I don't blame you Rita," said Julie.

Chapter 3

They were taking advantage of a break between showers. Rita and Julie were sitting in the garden of Julie's home having a chat. In another part of the garden the children were playing, accompanied by Yansis and Vinny who had left their seats to join in the fun.

Rita heard a commotion at the far end of the garden followed by Daniel's screeching. While Julie turned around in her seat, Rita leant to one side so she could see behind Julie who was sitting opposite her. This afforded Rita an extended view of Yansis and Vinny chasing the children while Daniel, Thomas and Emily squealed with excitement.

"We're the Tickle Monsters," shouted Vinny, in as scary a voice as he could muster. "We're coming to get you, and when we catch you, we're going to tickle you."

Yansis let out a loud roar, and they both pursued the children, with hands raised and fingers splayed.

"They're as bad as the kids, aren't they?" said Julie, turning back to face Rita.

"Never mind," laughed Rita. "At least it keeps the kids happy. Daniel, Thomas and Emily seem to be enjoying it too."

A few moments of silence passed between them. Rita became pensive, running through the events of the previous day yet again. Julie was quick to pick up on her mood.

"Are you still worrying about what your aunty said?" she asked.

"What, Aunty Irene? A bit, yeah. She's a spiteful old cow who seems to enjoy stirring up trouble, but I'm worried about Raeni too."

"Well, what do you want to do about it, Reet? Y'know, I suppose you could always take Daniel to see Raeni. It might just put your mind at …"

Julie didn't get a chance to finish what she was saying. "No fuckin' chance!" Rita snapped. "Not after what happened to our Jenny. Have you forgotten all the shit I went through?"

"Yeah but, it's just …"

"No way am I taking Daniel to see her. It's not happening, not in my fuckin' lifetime anyway! I couldn't go through all that again. Daniel's staying with me and Yansis, where I know he's safe. I'm not letting him go anywhere near Leroy's family."

Julie remained silent, choosing instead to turn and watch the children again. In the silence that followed, Rita's mind began to wander. A mental image resurfaced. She and Yansis. Kneeling over the body. Feeling for a pulse. Blood clinging to their hands and clothing. Blood on the body. Blood on the carpet. Blood everywhere!

She could feel her heart rate speed up as she pictured Jenny before they had taken her to hospital. Five years ago, yet the memory was as vivid as if it was yesterday. Rita could almost smell the excrement from the dead bodies that had littered the room. She tried to clear her mind but it wouldn't go away.

The sound of Julie's voice made her jump. "Bloody hell, Rita," she said, as she turned to face her. "You're edgy, aren't you? Are you sure you're OK? You've gone really pale."

"What? Yeah sure, I'm fine."

Rita didn't want to share the thoughts that were troubling her, not even with her best friend, Julie. She didn't like to cause overdue concern. She'd coped with the flashbacks before, and they'd gone away eventually.

She couldn't understand why they had returned after such a long time. But she guessed it was something to do with being back in Manchester. The place where her sister died. And concerns over Daniel weren't helping, especially in view of Raeni's feelings on the subject, and what her aunty had said.

"Stop worrying about everything," said Julie. "If you don't want to take Daniel to see Raeni, nobody can force you. She has no rights over him."

"I know, I know, it's just … bad memories, that's all."

Julie covered Rita's hand with hers, "I understand. But it's all in the past, Rita, and nobody can harm any of you now."

Rita forced a smile. Julie was right. It was just her imagination playing tricks on her. She needed to put it to the back of her mind and try to enjoy her visit. Providing they stayed away from the Riverhill, nobody could harm them. After all, nobody even knew where they were.

***

Wednesday 12th June 1996

They led Maurice James past the cells while the other prisoners were locked in. Two burly officers flanked him. The prisoners knew who he was. As soon as he stepped outside the first cell, the disturbance began. Hissing and yelling abuse. 'Beast' and 'fuckin' monster' were among the words used.

Then they walked him across the prison yard. The commotion built to a climax. Angry faces glared through the windows, huge fists were waved and instruments were banged against the cell walls and doors. Maurice kept his head down low, avoiding eye contact with his accusers. The officers ignored the disruption, which would die down once he was processed and released.

When the officers delivered him to the relevant area, and handed him over to another officer, they left. Maurice looked at the officer whose job it was to deal with his release.

"Name and number?" asked the officer.

Maurice gave him the requested information and watched him enter some data onto a computer screen, take up his keys and open a locker. His manner was professional and detached, but Maurice suspected that he detested him as much as the prisoners did. He could tell by his body language; all the little signs that Maurice had learnt how to spot.

The officer plonked a package on the desk in front of him and handed an envelope to Maurice. "This is your discharge grant," he said, handing the envelope over. Then, nodding towards the package, he added, "These are what you came in with. Changing area's over there."

The clothes looked alien to Maurice; it was so long since he'd worn them. For the last five years he'd been used to prison issue clothing, which he now removed and cast aside, slowly, reluctantly, as though removing his protective armour. He'd remained in segregation during his time in prison to protect him from the other prisoners. But now he had to face the world, fearful of what awaited him on the outside.

To his consternation the clothes no longer fitted. While he'd been behind bars, he'd transitioned into early middle age, and he had the paunch to show for it. To preserve his modesty, he put the prison garments back on before approaching the officer.

"They're too tight."

An imperceptible grin grazed the officer's lips. "Try the

box over there. Here's a bag to put your stuff in if you want to take it home with you," he said, placing a plastic carrier bag on the desk.

Maurice approached the box, a large open container full of dusty garments. He pulled them out, one by one, checking them for size and quality. All second-hand, he guessed, as he rejected each in turn.

"Come on, we haven't got all day!" shouted the officer. "I've got other prisoners to process."

Maurice settled for a pair of jeans with the button missing, and a sweatshirt, which was faded round the cuffs. He grabbed his old belt, hoping it still fit so the jeans would stay up.

After a few minutes, he emerged from the changing area wearing the shabby outfit. It was his final humiliation, courtesy of HM Prison Service. The officer didn't say another word as he unlocked the doors and led Maurice to the prison gates.

Maurice stepped outside Strangeways Prison clutching his release papers. He was thankful to be on the other side of the prison walls despite his trepidation. He clung on to his meagre possessions, placing his release papers inside the bag, out of view.

Then he headed towards the centre of Manchester. As he progressed along Bury New Road he cast his eyes back to the imposing nineteenth-century building, its ventilation tower standing tall and foreboding, acting as a bleak beacon of the evil contained within.

After five years inside, he viewed his release with a mixture of relief and apprehension. At least he would no longer be forever worried about the threat from other prisoners. The constant fear that he would be got at, like those poor buggers in the riots of '90. And to think, they called his sort animals. The things the other inmates would do to him if they ever got their hands on him; it didn't bear thinking about.

He'd served out the last two years of a five-year stretch at Strangeways, now known as HM Prison Manchester since it reopened in 1994. If it hadn't been for the prison shutting after the riots, he could have served the whole of his term there.

Now that his sentence was behind him, he could live in relative liberty, although he knew that he would never really be free. For a start, he was under the supervision of his probation officer, which meant that he had to report regularly. Fair enough, the PO had got him fixed up with somewhere to live, but subject to certain conditions.

Apart from the probation service, the housing people would want to make sure he didn't step out of line. Then there were the police. He knew from experience that they would haul him in for questioning whenever the opportunity arose.

Still, according to his probation officer he should be grateful. He had somewhere to live, which was better than living on the streets. Having an address meant he could also sign on. And it wasn't a million miles away, within easy reach of the centre of Manchester too.

He looked down at the piece of paper with the address written on it. Yes, he just needed to get to Piccadilly now so he could find out which bus to catch. He continued down Bury New Road towards Deansgate in the city centre. As he walked along, he planned his cover story ready for when he met his new neighbours on the Riverhill Estate in Longsight.

After a good fifteen to twenty-minute walk, Maurice reached Piccadilly Gardens and sat down on a bench. He took time to rest before he set about finding which bus to catch to the Riverhill. It was a warm, sunny day and he decided to take advantage of it; after all, he hadn't seen much sunshine during his time inside.

He sat there breathing in the city air and absorbing everything around him: the greenery, the bright flower beds, people rushing about their business. It all seemed so new and different. He was clammy from his walk and he gazed across at the fountain in the middle of the gardens. So welcoming and inviting. But adults didn't jump under fountains; not in the centre of Manchester, anyway. And he didn't want to do anything that would make him stand out.

He noticed some children racing around the fountain and squealing with glee as their lithe little bodies enjoyed the cool sprays of water. Maurice envied their ability to do as they pleased. He continued watching them lasciviously. It was OK to look; no one could stop him looking. As long as he didn't touch.

Chapter 4

Wednesday 12th June 1996 - Evening

"Where you goin' at this time of night, Jamal?" asked Raeni, her rich Jamaican accent still evident after more than thirty years in the UK.

"Out."

"Out where?"

"What's it matter? What's your problem? I'm twenty-two, for fuck's sake! I don't have to tell you everywhere I go."

"Don't you come at me with that language! I'll tell you my problem," Raeni replied, her voice rising. "My problem is what you gettin' up to at eleven o'clock at night. I wouldn't have no problem if it wasn't for the police at my door night and day asking their questions. And what's that you got in your hands?"

"Chicken, why?"

"My God! That's our tea for tomorrow," said Raeni, eying the chicken drumsticks that Jamal was devouring. She had spiced and cooked enough for two meals, saving money on a bulk purchase. The remainder she had intended to add to a casserole the following day. "What am I going to do now?" she asked.

"I dunno, get some more or summat. God, woman, you need to chill."

Raeni knew it wouldn't be as easy as that. There wasn't much food in the house, and she couldn't buy any more until her benefits were due. She supposed she would have to go scrounging to the neighbours again.

"I can't get no more, I've got no money. And you speak to me with a bit more respect, boy!"

But she was wasting her time. Jamal was already out of the door, slamming it behind him as he left. His behaviour was becoming more erratic and she was convinced he was taking drugs. Although lots of young men rebelled, Jamal's behaviour was outside the norm, and she worried about him constantly. Raeni turned to her other son, Devan, who hadn't been home long himself and had sneaked in looking suspicious.

"What's going on, Devan? What's he up to?"

"I don't know, do I?"

"You boys will be the death of me. All you bring me is worry every day. I been through this already with Leroy. No good will come of it. Are you listening to me, boy?"

Devan was busy thumbing through the keys on the TV remote control so Raeni prodded him to get his attention.

"What?" he shouted, backing away but glaring aggressively at her.

"Don't ignore me when I'm talking to you. Where you been tonight, anyway?"

"Out with my mates."

"Well I hope you haven't been up to no good."

"Give it a rest, will you? I'm sick of hearing it."

Raeni knew it was no use. If she pursued the matter, it would only result in a row, and Devan wasn't the worst of her worries. Jamal was causing her the most concern so it wasn't really fair to take it out on Devan. A row was the last thing she needed; it would be hard enough to sleep as it was. She knew she'd be tossing and turning half the night wondering what Jamal was up to, and expecting the police to come knocking on the door at any minute. Defeated, she went up to bed and left Devan watching the TV.

***

Thursday 13th June 1996 - Evening

John examined his equipment one last time. Dressed in full kit, he was ready to go out on a raid at a drugs den in Harpurhey. He tested the strapping that held the holster for his Glock handgun around his thigh, made sure his body armour was securely in place, and checked that he was carrying a good supply of ammunition in the compartments fastened round his torso. Then he checked his shotgun once more.

"It's the bloody waiting I can't stand," he said to his colleague and best friend, Tony. "I'm hyped up and ready to go. I just want to get it over with, now."

"I know what you mean, mate. I'm well psyched up to sort the bastards."

"Only if we're under threat though, eh Tony?"

"Oh yeah, course. I know the bloody protocol by now, John. I just mean, get the job done."

John smiled ironically at his friend's familiar zeal. "Just checkin', that's all."

"I know, but you know as well as I do, John, they don't call us in unless there's a threat. A lot of these dealers are tooled up these days. Fuckin' would-be gangsters, that's the trouble with 'em. If it comes down to it, I won't hesitate. It's them or me, and I'm not losing my life to some low-life scum because I'm trying to talk him round when he pulls a gun on me. Fuckin' deserve all they get."

John didn't respond to his friend's rant. He could have said that a lot of the 'would be gangsters' were just kids who'd taken the wrong path in life, but he would have been perceived as weak and that wouldn't do. In this job you had to have confidence in each other, and know that you had each other's backs should the need arise.

He understood Tony's point of view but wished he wasn't

so blasé about the possible loss of life. Like his friend, Tony, John would also do what needed to be done; they both knew that. But it didn't stop him feeling bad about it.

He thought back to the young lad in Iraq, then swiftly tried to dispel the memory from his mind. Now wasn't the time for thoughts like that when he was due out on a raid. He had to stay focused so he could remain impassive if a threat occurred. That way he could carry out the job he was trained to do, without hesitation.

They were different, him and Tony. He didn't always agree with Tony's views but, apart from his overzealousness in the face of opposition, Tony was a great guy. They had spent time together in the forces, and it was Tony who had given him the tip off about Greater Manchester Police recruiting for a special task force.

It came at just the right moment, when he had grown tired of spending time away. He was getting no younger and was becoming ready to settle down. Thankfully he met Paula, his soulmate, not long after he returned home.

While they were waiting, an attractive, twenty-something Detective Constable called Janet walked through the office, and Tony gave John a meaningful glance.

"Morning lads," she greeted. "You look ready for action."

"Always ready, me," Tony quipped.

Janet gave a flirtatious giggle as she made eye contact with John, then continued past them.

Once she was out of earshot, Tony grinned and said, "If you ask me, she's still up for a repeat performance, mate."

"No chance," said John. "That's all in the past, and that's where it's staying."

Tony was referring to a brief fling that John had with Janet not long after he joined the police force. But it hadn't lasted, despite Janet's enthusiasm. John soon realised that the relationship didn't have long-term potential. So they'd remained good friends, and agreed to keep it that way. Then he'd met Paula, and he knew within weeks that she was the one.

"Oy, daydreamer!" shouted Tony, breaking John out of his reverie. "It looks like we're set to go. Here comes Smithson to give us the OK."

***

Thursday 13th June 1996 - Evening
They were instructed to raid a third-floor flat. When they received the order to enter the premises, John, Tony and several other officers rammed down the door and charged inside. As soon as John was inside the property, the pungent smell of cannabis hit him.

While other officers raced through the flat, John and Tony took the first room they came to, accompanied by two other officers. They dashed inside, ready to arrest the occupants and seize any illegal drugs.

John gave the usual command, "Police, stay where you are!"

There were five people already in the room: three men and two women, all in their early twenties. John approached them, prepared for resistance, but, unlike other raids, the occupants remained calm and unflinching.

The five people were seated around a coffee table on gaudy beanbags and cushions, forming a circle. In the centre of the circle, the focus of their attention was a large bong mounted proudly on the coffee table. One of the men was taking a hit from the bong while the others waited for their turn.

"Stop what you're doing!" ordered Tony, pointing his

Glock in the man's direction.

To John's amazement, the man continued to inhale deeply from the bong. John stepped in and grabbed the bong. The man staggered back onto his cushion, his face a picture of pure indulgence as the cannabis entered his system.

"Cuff 'em!" ordered the sergeant who had just stepped into the room.

John and the rest of the team carried out their orders. The men and women allowed themselves to be led outside, their bodies slack and their manner impassive. John flashed Tony a knowing look, as he realised that their detainees were so stoned that they were indifferent to their fate.

Once they had them in the van, John left two officers guarding them while he went to check out the rest of the flat.

"Take a butcher's at the middle room," said one of his colleagues.

As John approached the room, the pungent, sweet stench of cannabis became stronger. Now he understood why he could smell it as soon as he entered the flat. The whole of the room was being used as a cannabis farm. Once he was inside, not only was the smell overbearing, but the heat and humidity were oppressive too.

It was a sophisticated set-up. The room was crammed full of pots containing cannabis plants, a sea of green with their pointed fern-shaped leaves protruding in every direction. John could feel the warmth from enormous lamps, which shone down onto the plants, flooding the room with their powerful rays.

Overhead, the ceiling was lined with foil, which reflected the light and heat, increasing the intensity. The windows were covered in sodden black canvas, and condensation streamed down the walls. Several fans were also attached to the walls.

"They've cut into the mains," said John's colleague, indicating the power source while John looked around the room in awe. "Is it the first one you've seen?"

"Yeah," said John. "It would be impressive if it wasn't so bloody stupid."

"I know. It's a pity they don't make better use of their talents."

"No wonder they were so stoned. There's enough here to keep all of Harpurhey going, I should think."

"Oh yeah, and by the look of it they've been doing a roaring trade. They've got a load of equipment in that other room. Looks like they've been drying and curing it, and then bagging it up to sell."

John was amazed at the operation, and couldn't wait to tell Tony who was sitting in a police car outside, waiting to take them back to the station. The detainees had already been taken in a police van. He related to Tony what he had found in the flat. To his surprise, Tony didn't share his incredulity as it wasn't the first time he'd seen a cannabis farm.

"It beats me why they called us in though," Tony commented. "They were hardly armed and dangerous, were they?"

John laughed. "There must have been a reason for it. Maybe there have been reports of violence or they were considered a threat or summat. But there were no firearms found in the property," he said.

"Oh well, at least it was a nice easy job. I wish every raid was as straightforward as that one."

"Yeah, but don't forget," said John. "It's the easy ones that prepare us for when things get really tough."

Chapter 5

Paula greeted Rita and Yansis enthusiastically when they arrived at the home she shared with Rita's brother, John. They lived in a three-bedroomed semi in Droylsden, a working-class area and former mill town about four miles east of the city centre. It was also more than three miles away from the Riverhill Estate, which suited John.

"John's in the back, just opening the wine," she said, causing Rita and Yansis to laugh as they held up a bottle each, one red and one white.

"Oh, you needn't have bothered, we've got plenty," said Paula.

They went through to the dining room and Rita gave John a hug. "Alright, little brother?" she asked.

Although John had inherited height from his father's side of the family, and towered above Rita, he was two years younger. She therefore liked to fondly refer to him as her 'little' brother.

"Hi Sis, hi Yansis. It's nice to meet you properly at last," said John, shaking Yansis's hand before addressing both of them by adding, "You didn't need to bring any wine, we've got loads."

"That's what I just told them," said Paula.

"Yeah, we got a bit carried away at the supermarket. We were spoilt for choice so we thought, sod it, we'll have the lot," said John.

Rita gazed around her appreciatively before commenting, "This is a nice place you've got."

"Thanks. We bought it a couple of years ago. It was in a

right state but we've done a lot of work on it, and Paula's pretty good at deciding what looks right." John then looked behind Rita and Yansis before asking, "No Daniel?"

"Oh no, we decided it was best to leave him at Julie's. He'll only get restless with a load of adults. Besides, he loves it there, and Julie and Vinny were happy to take him off our hands. Anyway, judging by the amount of booze you've bought, I don't think we'll be in any fit state to look after him," Rita laughed.

They sat down to dinner. Paula took care of the food, and seemed to be a dab hand in the kitchen. She had prepared a Chinese meal for them with mixed starters, and three dishes for the main course. While she served up the food, John sorted out the drinks, pouring Rita and Yansis a generous glass of wine each.

Noting the enormous glasses, Rita commented, "Bloody hell, John, are you trying to get us drunk, or what?"

"Don't worry, Rita. I will carry you home," laughed Yansis.

"Aye, that's if you're in a fit state yourself."

The meal got off to a good start with all four of them getting along well together. Rita chatted away to Paula who was eager to find out all about their life in Greece, while John and Yansis got to know each other.

"You'll both have to come and visit us in Greece," said Rita. "You're welcome to stay anytime."

"Yes, that's right," agreed Yansis.

"Oh, thank you. It sounds lovely," said Paula. "We might just take you up on the offer."

Then Rita and John began to share family banter, amusing Paula and Yansis with stories of their childhood.

Rita and Yansis were enjoying themselves so much that they didn't realise how frequently John was topping up their glasses. By the time they finished eating they were all the worse for wear.

"That was a nice meal, Paula. You're a brilliant cook. I'm so full I can hardly move."

"Thank you, I'm glad you enjoyed it. We don't have to get up yet. Stay a bit longer; there's no rush."

They were having such a good time, they didn't want the evening to end. So, rather than retiring into the living room or calling a taxi home, they remained at the dining table drinking more wine and chatting.

When the drink was running out, John went into the kitchen to fetch more. He returned with a tray containing another two bottles of wine, four brandy glasses and a bottle of brandy.

"Come on, let's have an after-dinner toast," he said, placing the brandy glasses on the table and pouring a liberal measure into each.

"Not for me," said Yansis. "I've already drunk too much."

"Oh, don't be miserable," coaxed Rita. "It's not every day I get to spend some time with my little brother and his new wife."

"Yeah, come on," giggled Paula who would have been wise to leave the brandy alone. "To brothers and sisters, no, no … to sisters-in-laws and brothers-in-in-law," she slurred.

They all raised their glasses in a drunken toast, then Rita and Yansis continued chatting to John. Meanwhile Paula sat giggling at something imagined that must have amused her.

"Anyway, little brother, you've not told us much about what you do," said Rita. "What's it like being in the police? Do you get to lock up many bad guys?" she teased.

Before John had a chance to reply, Paula made an ill-advised and hasty response, "Oh yeah, he sorts out all the bad guys." Then she lowered her voice, whispering in the exaggerated way that drunken people do, "Gangsters."

Rita immediately reacted on hearing the word 'gangsters', remembering how her sister had died at the hands of a ruthless gang a few years prior. "What do you mean?" she asked, responding to Paula's statement but looking at John.

"Firearms," said Paula. "That's what he does." Then she hiccupped and dropped back out of the conversation, sitting with her head lolling to one side.

Rita raised her eyebrows questioningly as she looked at John, noting the look of annoyance he flashed at Paula.

"I think I'd best get Paula a glass of water," he said, getting up to leave the table.

But Rita wasn't put off so easily, and when he returned she resumed the conversation.

"What's going on, John?"

"Nothing, it's not what you think … You think I'm on some bloody revenge mission or summat, but I'm not. It's not like that. It's just coincidence."

"Quite a big coincidence, John."

Yansis was gently tugging her top to get her to hold back but she wasn't prepared to give up.

"Look," said John. "They were looking for guys who were used to handling guns to set up a special task force to tackle gun crime. Obviously those who have been in the army are ideal because they've already had the training. I wanted to leave the forces and settle back home and I needed a secure job, so I thought, why not."

"And do you … shoot gangsters?"

"Rita, I don't shoot anyone if I can help it. I shouldn't even be talking to you about this. Paula shouldn't have said anything."

Paula lifted her head on hearing her name, but when she realised no one was expecting a response from her, she let it droop again.

"Look, I think it's best I get Paula up to bed," said John.

"OK," said Rita.

While John was putting Paula to bed, Yansis said, "Rita, I think it is getting very late. We should get ready to go."

"In a bit, Yansis. I just want to talk to John a bit longer first." She took a large swig of her brandy as she waited for her brother to return.

After a few minutes, John entered the dining room. The atmosphere had now changed between them. The jollity of the evening was replaced by solemnity at the reminder of how their sister died. However, they were still very drunk so Rita wasn't as subtle as she might otherwise have been.

When John joined them at the table, she asked, "Have you ever killed anyone, John?"

"Yes, but only if I've been put in a situation where it's them or me. I've only done it if it's been absolutely necessary."

"Have you any regrets?"

"Rita, this is not nice," said Yansis. "I think it is time for us to go."

"No, it's OK," said John. "We've started this now so we might as well finish it. I'm not an animal Rita. I don't kill for the sake of it. And yes, of course I have regrets, two big ones, actually."

Rita could see that John was getting a little emotional and she decided not to push him any further, but just as she thought John wasn't going to say anymore, he continued.

"Most of the time I don't regret it. You can't afford to; it's what you're trained to do. You just have to view it as part of the job. But there was one. He was young, too young. I had no choice; it was either him or me. Still doesn't make me feel any better though. It's one thing taking them out at long

39

range, but this guy was only a couple of metres away …"

He broke off and looked into his glass where he nervously swirled the brandy around before taking a long, hard swig.

"What was your other regret?" asked Rita.

"God, you haven't changed, have you Sis? You don't bloody give up, do you?"

"OK, OK, I'm sorry, I shouldn't have asked. I've had too much to drink."

"It's alright, you might as well know." Rita could see him getting emotional, his eyes tearing up as the alcohol relinquished his control. "My other regret is that while I was away doing my duty for Queen and country, some bastard here was shooting my sister. I should have been here protecting her. Maybe if I'd have been home, I could have saved her. I might have been able to warn her about what she was getting herself into."

"Don't be so bleedin' daft," Rita snapped as Yansis gripped John's shoulder in a gesture of reassurance. "You can't blame yourself. There was nothing anyone could have done. I should know that; I tried hard enough to get her away from him. She chose her partner and the consequences that went with that. She must have had an idea from the start that he was bad news, but you know what Jenny was like. She always ran with the wrong crowd."

John now had his head bowed down and had resorted to staring aimlessly into his brandy glass.

There were a few moments of silence while they were all immersed in their own thoughts. Then Rita, knowing what she needed to say, and plucking up the courage to do so, took a deep breath before speaking again, "There's just one thing I need to know, John … that you won't do anything stupid because of what happened to Jenny."

"No, of course I won't! That's not why I joined the task

force. I hope I never have to shoot anyone again. We mostly have the guns for self-protection and to act as a deterrent. But if push came to shove, and I had to do it, then I would."

Rita accepted his explanation. Although, deep down, she was still a little concerned about his motivations, she took his word for it. And she believed him when he said he didn't have any ulterior motive in taking the job.

***

Saturday 15ᵗʰ June 1996 - Morning

When Paula came downstairs the following morning, John planted a kiss on her cheek.

"Ooh, watch my head, it's throbbing," she said.

"I'm not surprised, with the amount you were throwing back last night."

"You can talk," she laughed.

Turning serious, he asked, "Do you realise you let the cat out of the bag?"

"What do you mean?"

"About my job; that I'm on the Special Task Force."

"Oh, that … I'm sorry. I'm not exactly subtle when I've had a few, am I? I'm sure it'll be OK though, John. She is your sister after all; they can be trusted."

"Yeah, but the only problem is, she thinks there's something dodgy about me taking on the job in the first place. She thinks I've taken it to get revenge for what happened to Jenny."

"Oh, yeah. I think I can remember her quizzing you before I went to bed. What did you tell them?"

"Everything. I guess I'd drunk too much as well."

"What exactly is 'everything'?"

"The young kid in Iraq, my regrets that I wasn't here for Jenny."

"Oh."

"Don't worry, I also told her that Jenny wasn't the reason I joined the task force. We both know it's true, but whether Rita believed me or not, I don't know."

"Don't let it bother you John. As long as your conscience is clear, that's all that matters."

Chapter 6

"Where are you lot off to?" asked Julie.

"I thought I'd show Yansis and Daniel the delights of Manchester City Centre," said Rita. Then, looking at Yansis, she added, "It's high time I introduced you to Manchester's biggest public toilet, Yansis. You don't know what you've been missing."

While Rita and Julie laughed, Yansis looked perplexed.

"Manchester Arndale," Rita explained. "It's a big shopping centre, but the press called it a giant public toilet when it first opened because the outside walls are covered in dingy yellow tiles. It's got some great shops though, so who cares what they used to build it?"

"Come on, Daniel. Let's get you ready," said Rita.

Daniel was glued to the TV set watching a Thomas the Tank Engine video with Julie's four-year-old son, Thomas. Since they'd arrived in the UK, Daniel had got along well with Julie's children. He was particularly close to Thomas who was nearer in age to him than seven-year-old Emily. Thomas introduced Daniel to the delights of Thomas the Tank Engine videos. The fact that the star engine bore Thomas's name added to the appeal, and Daniel was impressed with this idea.

"Aaw, please can I stay and play with Thomas? I don't want to go to a toilet."

Rita, Julie and Yansis laughed at Daniel's innocent remark. "We're not going to a toilet. Mummy was only joking. We're going into Manchester where there are lots of shops. Thomas is going to see his grandma and granddad."

"Please can I go to see Giagiá and Pappoús?"

Rita smiled, aware that Daniel was referring to Yansis's parents, and using the Greek for Grandma and Granddad. As Daniel regarded Rita and Yansis as his parents, as far as he was aware, Yansis's parents were therefore his grandparents. He'd spent almost all of his life in Greece so he was used to Yansis's parents, but this was his first visit to the UK.

At five years of age, he didn't fully understand the concept of travel so he couldn't appreciate that it wasn't just a matter of popping round to his Greek grandparents and then back in time for tea. She tried to explain to him, as gently as she could, that they would be in the UK for a while, and that he would have plenty of time with his grandparents once they returned to Greece.

"Well, can I wait for Thomas?" he asked, not yet sold on the idea of going shopping.

"No, cheeky. There'll be no one here to look after you. Anyway, Thomas will be here when you get back and if you're a good boy, we might get you a treat."

"Ooh, what is it?"

"You'll have to wait and see. It's a surprise."

Rita smiled fondly at her son. He had brought her and Yansis such pleasure over the years, and now he was turning into a proper little character. Daniel was at the inquisitive age when he was full of curiosity about the world around him. He was constantly asking questions and trying to put things into a context that his five-year-old mind could interpret. His endless thirst for knowledge and frequent misunderstandings caused them much amusement, and he had boundless energy and an enthusiasm that was infectious.

The promise of a treat did the trick, especially when Daniel saw that Thomas was, in fact, leaving the house.

Julie's home then lost its appeal and Daniel became eager to join his parents on their trip to the city centre.

"Right, before we go, you need to have your inhaler," said Rita.

She took Daniel's large nebuhaler and inserted his inhaler in the aperture at one end, then attached the facial mask to the other end before gently placing the mask over Daniel's face. When Rita pressed the inhaler, Daniel knew what was required of him and he kept the mask over his face to a count of ten to allow all the asthma medication from the nebuhaler to reach his airways.

"That's a good boy," said Rita. "Right, now let's get your shoes on."

She bent to tie his shoelace, then sat up straight to face him again. "How's that?"

Daniel smiled, and she waited for his reply. As she looked into his eyes, she pictured her sister, Jenny, the last time she saw her alive.

Attempting to speak. Struggling to utter her final words. Rita talking to her. Waffling about their childhood, grandparents, food, anything. Trying to keep her awake. Trying to keep her alive. The blood. The smell.

Then everyone seemed to speak at once.

Daniel: "They're fine, Mummy."

Julie: "Are you OK, Rita? You don't look well."

Yansis: "What is the matter?"

"Oh sorry, I was miles away," said Rita, rushing to reassure them while Julie and Yansis appeared concerned. She brushed the incident aside while she continued to focus on Daniel.

Once they were ready, Rita and Yansis set off, accompanied by one excited little boy who was looking forward to finding out what treat was awaiting him.

Yansis waited until they were outside before he asked. "It is happening again, isn't it?"

"Yes, but don't worry. I'm OK."

She flashed a warning look from him to Daniel.

"When did it start?"

"A few days ago. I think it's just 'cos we're back in Manchester. But I'm not having as many as last time. I'm sure they'll go once we're home."

"You should have told me, Rita."

"I didn't want to make a fuss. It was bound to happen when you think about it; it *was* traumatic when all's said and done."

"Mummy, what's drawmatic?" asked Daniel.

"Nothing, Love. It's just grown-up talk. Nothing for you to worry about." She glared at Yansis.

"OK," he said. "We'll talk about it later."

***

Saturday 15th June 1996 - Morning
Maurice picked up one of the soft toys he had arranged in a neat line on the upstairs landing: a white cuddly bear. He put it inside a plastic carrier bag before leaving his house. It was three days since he moved into his new abode and, while it wasn't ideal, it was an improvement on the place he had called home for the past few years.

The house was bereft of furniture, apart from a few items, and other comforts were lacking. Still, that would come in time but, for now, he would seek his comforts outside the home.

He decided to go to the local park. Maurice had already found out where it was by asking his neighbour, on the pretence of wanting to take his niece when she came to visit.

As he walked through the streets, he noticed how run-down the estate was. Front doors opened onto homes that emitted malodorous stenches.

Although it was still only around 9 a.m., a few of the doors were left unlocked so restless young children could pass in and out without disturbing their parents. He caught sight of the interior of one such dwelling, the paint stained and peeling and the wallpaper torn.

An overweight woman with bleached blonde hair and dark roots was sitting inside the property, facing outwards, on the pretence of watching the kids, he supposed. She was smoking a roll-up and chuckling at something indoors that was amusing her and was commanding far more of her attention than her children. He watched the tatty little urchins playing outside; aged no more than four and roaming in and out of the house at will. You'd think their parents would be more careful.

On the way to the park he passed by the local supermarket, situated on a small shopping precinct where, later in the day, youths hung about in gangs, clowning around and causing a nuisance. Naturally cautious near groups of young males, he would always stiffen on approaching them.

Relief flooded through him when he saw that there were no youths hanging around. At this time in the morning they would still be in bed. For now it should be relatively safe to venture out for his shopping, and he made a mental note to collect a few items on his way back. He couldn't help but wonder how different things would be if people ever found out about his history.

As he progressed through the precinct, Maurice encountered occasional globules of yellowy green mucus stuck to the ground. Its consistency was so thick and slimy that it took several downpours of rain to wash it away. Catarrh: a product of pollution, cheap cigarettes and poor diet.

Maurice trudged along, kicking up greasy paper wrappings that had spilt from the overflowing bin outside the fish and chip shop. The wind had blown litter against a small wall surrounding a bogus raised border. Its upper area was now a failed garden full of barren bushes, downtrodden weeds, cigarette butts and the occasional used condom. Among the litter, flies fed hungrily on dog faeces and discarded chips spilling from a carton.

He continued on past the end shop, a bookie's. Curiosity made him glance inside; it was the busiest shop on the precinct, crowded, dark and fuggy with the haze of exhaled cigarette smoke and cannabis hanging in the air.

This was his sort of area: a place where the menacing and the vulnerable co-existed.

As he moved away from the precinct, the roads became wider and busier. Many of the run-down houses gave way to other buildings: pubs, car showrooms and warehouses. After walking for ten more minutes he spotted it: a verdant oasis amongst the urban decay. He felt the thrill of excitement pulsate through him in anticipation.

A new park. New opportunities. New challenges. He took his seat on a bench, which he had selected for its prime view of the children's play area. And then he watched.

Two young girls in matching outfits played in the sandpit, chatting amicably in their make-believe world. He wondered if they were alone but doubted it. They were too clean, too polished. Girls in matching outfits didn't come to the park alone, not like the kids he'd passed in the street who would be coming here unaccompanied as soon as they could find their way.

Further back from them a small boy took repeated turns on the slide, "Look at me, Mummy."

A woman's voice called back in response, and Maurice traced the location of the voice. It was coming from a lady who was sitting on the other side of the play area with a female friend. Soon enough, a playmate joined the boy. Maurice assumed he was the other woman's son.

At the opposite end of the bench to the two women was an elderly lady, and Maurice wondered if she was looking after the two young girls. This was confirmed when one of them ran to the lady who gave her a carton of drink. There was only one other child in the playground. A man was pushing him on the swing; presumably he was his father.

None of the children in this park were alone apart from some much older children who were playing football on a nearby field. That fact surprised him, considering the feral state of the children he had passed on the estate, and he wondered whether there was another housing area somewhere close to the park.

While the old lady was occupied with one of the girls, the other girl continued making sandcastles and chattering to herself. Maurice withdrew the white teddy bear from his plastic bag and bounced it up and down on his knee. This gained the girl's attention; the bright white of the bear's fur distracted her and she looked up. Maurice smiled, and she wandered towards him, slowly at first but faster when Maurice took the bear's paws between his fingers and mimed a dance for the little girl's delectation.

"What's he called?" she asked when she reached Maurice.

"Snowy," said Maurice, "because he's so white, and he likes dancing in the snow."

He mimed another dance with the bear and the young girl rewarded him with a smile then put out her hand to stroke

Snowy's head.

"Can I play with him?"

"Only if you're good."

Before Maurice had a chance to elicit a further response from the girl, he was disturbed by the sound of the old lady shouting, "Jessica, Jessica, come back here!"

She trundled off and Maurice noticed the two other women peering over at him and whispering among themselves. He didn't dash off straightaway. That would have been too obvious. It was far better to stay there for a few minutes as though waiting for someone. He feigned looking at his watch a few times. Then, when he thought it was safe to do so, he sneaked away.

He had only wanted to look; he couldn't risk anything else. The trouble was there were always suspicious people about. He was just about to make his way home when a thought occurred to him. When his neighbour had described the park, he said it was near the hospital. Maurice ran through the neighbour's directions in his head and decided to give it a shot. He could always check with a passer-by and make sure he was heading in the right direction.

Within a few minutes, Maurice reached Manchester General Hospital. It was nearer than he thought and easy to find. Once he arrived, Maurice made straight for paediatrics. He went through the doors and into the corridors surrounding the children's ward with ease.

Maurice passed a couple of uniform-clad staff on the way, but they eyed the soft toy he was carrying and left him to go about his business. The only response he received was a look of pity from a lady as she passed him. She must have assumed he was the father of a sick child. Perfect! He didn't know why he hadn't thought of this before.

Just outside the children's ward was a quadrangle that he

surmised was used as an outdoor play area for those children who were well enough. He positioned himself in the corridor, standing at a window overlooking the quadrangle.

Adjacent to the corridor, and on his left, was another corridor leading into the ward, and across from him was the children's ward itself. On his right was an indoor play area, and from his position at the window he could see across the quadrangle and inside it.

Maurice remained there for good while, undisturbed. Staff came and went as well as parents with other youngsters who he assumed were the siblings of sick children.

While he stood there he practised looking forlorn. Occasionally someone would slow down on approaching him, their concern evident. When they did so, he would turn, head bowed and shoulders stooped, sniff and then turn back towards the window. In fact, when anybody came near, he would just adopt his saddest expression.

It was so easy. The soft toy made a convincing prop and, to anybody passing by, he was the heartbroken father of a very sick child. And nobody wanted to probe.

Eventually, he returned home. By that time the hospital was becoming busy, but Maurice assumed it was typical for a Saturday. He whistled to himself on his journey home. In a better mood than when he set off, he decided he would visit the children's ward another day. It might be just the tonic he needed. In fact, he might even go tomorrow.

Chapter 7

Saturday 15th June 1996

When they approached the city centre, Rita told Yansis to head for Deansgate first. She was determined to show Yansis and Daniel as much of the centre of Manchester as they could manage in one day. Therefore, she decided that by parking the car near to Deansgate, they could work their way from there, down Market Street and onto the Arndale Centre. That would enable them to take in the shops along Deansgate and Market Street as well. Then, after stopping for some lunch, they could walk back again.

They turned left onto the Mancunian Way, skirting around the outside of the busiest part of the city centre. Finding their way to Deansgate was straightforward enough but finding a parking space was another matter.

Traffic was building up when they reached Deansgate and it was proving difficult to park anywhere near the city centre. Rita guessed that there must have been an accident when she spotted several ambulances. They eventually found somewhere to park but it was about a fifteen-minute walk from the shops.

As they walked into town they noticed a helicopter circling in the distance, and Rita knew that usually meant the police were surveying something. When they arrived at Kendal's department store on Deansgate, they were surprised to see hordes of people milling around.

"I wonder what the hell's going on," said Rita. "There must be a march or a demonstration or summat."

Noticing that there was a heavy presence of police and other emergency personnel, Rita glanced around her, curious.

"Hang on here a minute, I'm just gonna ask that copper what's going on," she said. "I'll take you in Kendal's after. You'll love it in there."

"It's OK," said Yansis. "Daniel wants to look in the windows anyway. It's very nice."

Rita smiled, watching her son point at something in Kendal's shop window and pull Yansis closer. Unaccustomed to a big city, Daniel was fascinated by the huge displays, and she was enjoying seeing the wonder on his lovely little face.

She turned, about to make her way across the road towards the police officer on the other side. Then she overheard someone in the crowd say something about a bomb scare. This piqued her curiosity even more.

Rita was halfway across when an enormous bang rang in her ears. It was so loud that it shook the ground beneath her, throwing her off her feet. The nearby buildings seemed to shift. Then, silence as the city reeled from the shock.

The silence was soon broken by a huge cacophony. Alarms and sirens blaring. People screaming. Debris falling. And windows shattering. Emergency personnel barked swift orders into their radios.

Rita scrambled back to her feet and stood unsteadily. She gazed about her, trying to make sense of what had just happened.

All around, people were either wandering aimlessly or had collapsed on the street. Covered in blood and shards of glass, many were crying and screaming for help.

As small fragments of glass struck Rita's face and arms, all she could think about was Yansis and Daniel who had been standing next to the shop window. She rushed towards them, stopping when she saw their frightened, bloody faces. Yansis was still holding Daniel's hand but they were now on the ground. Daniel was crying out in distress.

"Oh my God!" shouted Rita as she made her way to them. "Are you OK?"

As it was a summer day, Yansis and Daniel were both wearing t-shirts and their arms, as well as their faces, were covered in blood.

"Help, we need some help!" urged Rita to a nearby security guard as she took in their appearance.

It was difficult to tell how badly cut they were; there was so much blood. The security guard seemed as stunned as they were. He was clutching the arm of an elderly lady who was weeping as a tide of crimson flowed down her face from a laceration to her head. Having led her from inside Kendal's, he looked around him, dazed, as though unsure what to do next.

He failed to notice Rita speak. She searched for someone else who could help but the emergency staff were all busy. In desperation, she kneeled over Daniel and tried to assess his wounds herself. The largest amount of blood was coming from his right arm. She rifled through her handbag for something she could use, and withdrew some tissues.

"Daniel, I need you to stay calm while I take care of your arm," she coaxed.

"Yes, do as mummy says," said Yansis, wincing with pain as the effort of speech made him aware of several cuts to his face.

Although Rita dabbed gently at Daniel's arm, he yelled, "No Mummy, it hurts!"

"I'm sorry love, try to be brave. I need to make it better."

Her trembling hand hovered over his damaged limb again, "Think of something nice, Daniel. Pretend you're on the beach at home."

Despite his pain and distress, Daniel attempted to smile

through his tears but his lips quivered. Rita cleaned up a lot of the blood revealing the worst of his wounds. It was a large open gash on his arm, which was pumping blood. She flinched as she caught sight of the raw, exposed flesh. She needed to close the wound. But what could she use? A tissue would break up and stick to it.

The thought of what she must do brought beads of sweat to Rita's forehead. Daniel would hate her for this. But there was no time to waste. Before she could change her mind, she tore a strip from the bottom of her flimsy summer top. She then ripped it in two. Using one half of the cloth, she grabbed both edges of the wound and held them tightly together.

Daniel's screams were heart-wrenching.

"Think of that beach love. Think of that beach. Sorry love, but it'll get better soon, I promise."

He writhed around, attempting to pull away, but Yansis helped to hold him firm. While grasping his wound, Rita held onto Daniel with her other hand, pulling him towards her. When he couldn't get away, he sunk his head into Rita's bosom where he howled with pain to the sound of Rita's thundering heartbeat.

Rita stemmed the flow of blood. She then used the remaining cloth to form a tourniquet, which she tied around Daniel's arm.

"There, it's done now, love," she said, planting a kiss on the top of his head.

"But it still hurts, Mummy," Daniel cried.

"I know, but we'll get some help soon. We'll find someone who can make it better."

She had been so preoccupied with Daniel that she hadn't examined Yansis's wounds properly. As she cuddled Daniel, she took a look at Yansis. Thankfully, his cuts didn't seem as deep as the one on Daniel's arm.

"What about you Rita? Are you cut badly?" asked Yansis.

"No, not too bad," she said, taking a quick glance at herself.

Suddenly, a noise from the building next to them drew their attention. They dashed out of the way, and Yansis swerved to avoid a piece of falling debris, which missed him by centimetres. Rita watched in horror as it crashed to the ground, shattering into tiny fragments. She was glad that Yansis's jeans protected his legs from the ricochet.

"Jesus! That was close. We need to get away from here," she said.

"No. Wait, Rita," said Yansis. "We don't know if it is safe. There may be other bombs."

A rush of fear seized her, and Rita could feel her heart thumping. As she observed the chaotic scene in the blood-soaked street, a feeling of panic threatened to overwhelm her. But she held it together, for Daniel.

It seemed to take forever until they could get anyone to help them. In the meantime, they tried to comfort Daniel. After a while, a police officer came to assess them. He told them to walk further up Deansgate where they would find ambulances ready to ferry injured people to hospital. Shaken from the event, they acted on the police officer's instructions. It wasn't so much a walk as a stagger because they were all still in a state of shock.

The air soon became dusty, which affected Daniel's asthma and he started coughing. Rita searched frantically inside her bag for his nebuhaler, before remembering they had left it in the car because it was too cumbersome to carry around.

As though sensing they didn't have his nebuhaler handy, Daniel soon became distressed and was panting for breath. Rita and Yansis stopped to give him a chance to get his breath back.

"Come on now, Daniel. Take deep breaths," said Rita, trying to keep Daniel calm. She glanced ahead, noticing the bank of ambulances in the distance. Realising that they were still some way off, she was finding it difficult to keep her own composure. The sight of Daniel panting and wheezing was upsetting.

"Come on, Daniel, nice big breaths," she repeated, but the uncertainty in her voice belied the encouragement she was trying to give Daniel.

"Like this, Daniel," said Yansis.

He then demonstrated, breathing deeply and sticking out his stomach in an exaggerated manner then letting his breath go slowly. Daniel copied his actions and for several minutes they stood on the pavement practising deep breathing. The passers-by were too consumed with their own troubles to bother about this unusual activity.

"Right, are we ready to go now?" asked Rita.

Before Daniel could object to the walk, Yansis lifted him up and put him on his back.

"But you're cut, Yansis," said Rita.

"It's OK. He's only light and it won't make any difference to my cuts."

Rita was full of admiration for Yansis as he struggled the rest of the way up Deansgate carrying Daniel.

"Just keep doing your deep breathing Daniel. We'll soon reach those ambulances there," she said, pointing. "Then a nice man or lady will give you something to help you feel better."

Once they arrived at the ambulances, Daniel was given oxygen and they were taken to Manchester General Hospital. It was a blow for Rita. The last time she visited hospital was when she lost her sister. In her haste to get help for Daniel and Yansis, she hadn't thought about the impact of a hospital visit. But as they approached the entrance, she could feel her heartbeat quickening as memories of her sister's death flooded her mind.

They staggered inside, dazed, and sat down among the many other injured people while the press pounced like pigeons foraging for scraps.

Any hopes of seeing an end to their suffering were soon shattered. The waiting room of the Accident and Emergency department was already packed and, as more casualties from the bombing arrived, the place became overcrowded. People smoked to calm their frayed nerves until a dense fug hung over the room. This exacerbated Daniel's breathing difficulties.

Although they were among the first casualties to arrive, they still had to wait two hours to be seen by a doctor in a department that was overworked and understaffed. The receptionist informed them on arrival that Daniel would be considered high priority due to his age and his asthma.

After a while Yansis lost his seat: there were too many people arriving whose need was greater. He joined lots of others who were forced to either stand or sit on the floor. Rita clung to her chair, nursing Daniel on her knee. She thought he was going through enough without having to endure the discomfort of the floor.

"My chest feels poorly, Mummy," Daniel complained, so Rita sent Yansis in search of a doctor.

"If they can't see him yet, ask them to let us have an inhaler, at least," she pleaded. "Will you ring my mam and Julie as well, and let them know what's happened please, Yansis?"

She passed Yansis her mobile, grateful that she had it. At least they weren't having to scout around for change, and then queue up to use the public phone, unlike many of those here.

As she sat waiting to be attended to, Rita watched a stream of people enter the waiting room. Bloody, bedraggled and distressed. Some were silent with shock. Others spoke in harried, clipped sentences, emitting shallow breaths between words of devastation. They repeated stilted, clichéd phrases: "I can't believe it!" "Oh my God!" "It's hell!" It was their only way to describe such a traumatic experience; their minds were too numbed to find other words.

It was several minutes before Yansis returned. "It is no good, Rita. All the doctors are busy with patients. I tried to wait till one was available, but a nurse told me to wait out here. She said Daniel will be seen as soon as possible."

Rita knew there was no point kicking up a fuss. The staff wouldn't see them any quicker. Besides, her conscience wouldn't allow her: some of the people here were in a much worse state.

"OK," she sighed. "Did you ring my mam and Julie?"

"Yes, I told Julie but your mother's phone was engaged."

"Thanks. I'll just have to try my mam again later if I get a chance."

In the end, Rita had no choice but to let Yansis keep their seat while she took Daniel outside for some air.

Rita wasn't comfortable about Daniel being a part of this situation either. Everywhere she looked there were people sick, in pain or bleeding. She was worried that Daniel would already be traumatised by the bomb, and being surrounded by so many bloody and distraught people would only make matters worse.

Aside from all that, they were fed up. There was nothing to do but listen to endless speculation about the bomb, or read out-of-date magazines. The latter was out of the question for Rita as she was busy looking after Daniel, and keeping him calm. Although Yansis offered to take over and give her a break, she thought Daniel needed her at the moment.

Unfortunately, with nothing to take Rita's mind off things, the impact of the bomb hit home. They were all suffering from delayed shock, and the thought of how much worse things could have been was preoccupying Rita.

She was thankful when Daniel's name was called out. Once they went through to the treatment rooms, a nurse assessed Daniel and provided more oxygen to ease his breathing until the doctor could get to him. When Rita saw some of the people who were waiting to see a doctor, she wasn't surprised that Daniel wasn't attended to first. She didn't envy the job of the staff who would have to decide the order of precedence among so many sick and injured.

The medical staff treated all three of them at the same time. Rita only had superficial wounds so it was just a matter of cleaning them up. Yansis and Daniel, on the other hand, had deeper cuts that needed stitches. Yansis went to have his cuts tended to while Rita stayed with Daniel. She held his hand to comfort him while he screamed as the doctor plunged the needle into him repeatedly.

When the doctor finished stitching Daniel, Rita heaved a sigh of relief, "Thank God for that. I just need to find my husband now so we can all go home," she said.

"I'm sorry but I think it's best if we don't send your son home just yet," said the doctor.

Rita looked at him in astonishment.

"Your son has suffered a great deal of distress and also inhaled a large amount of dust. In view of the fact that he is asthmatic, I would prefer to keep him in overnight for observation. There's nothing to worry about. It's just a precaution, but it's best to be on the safe side. He's one of the youngest victims of the bomb blast, and shock can do strange things to people."

"Oh … right. I-I'll let my husband know so we can fetch his pyjamas and stuff."

"If you want to stay with your son for now, I can go and let your husband know," volunteered a helpful nurse on seeing the look of dismay on Rita's face. "Don't worry about pyjamas. It's only for one night; I'm sure he'll manage with a hospital gown."

"Y-yeah, thank you," said Rita, her voice breaking.

She could feel a lump forming in her throat, and knew that the staff would see her reaction as a little extreme. But she couldn't help it. She didn't want Daniel to stay in hospital, but she was too concerned about him to go against the doctor's advice.

Although the doctor told her not to worry, she wasn't reassured. She didn't want to come to hospital in the first place, not after what happened to Jenny. However, she had regarded it as a quick patch up and then home, and that thought had kept her going. But the idea of her son staying overnight was too much. And, once again, memories of her dying sister flooded her mind.

"Will I be able to stay with him tonight?" she asked.

"I'm sorry but I'm afraid that won't be possible. There aren't enough beds. We're full to capacity at the moment because of the bomb blast," said the doctor. Then, seeing the expression on Rita's face, he gave her shoulder a reassuring squeeze before adding, "Don't worry, my nurses will look after him well. He'll be absolutely fine. If you can wait here with Daniel, one of the staff will let you know when we have a bed ready on the ward."

Then he was gone before Rita could say anything more.

When Yansis returned, Rita gabbled, "He's got to stay in overnight because of his asthma." Her voice was shaking. "They won't let me stay. They said there's not enough beds."

"I'm sure it is for the best," said Yansis. "The doctors know what they are doing."

"I'm not leaving him on his own!" Rita snapped. "If there's not enough beds then I'll just have to sleep in a bloody visitor's chair."

Yansis sat down next to her and took her hands in his, "Rita, calm down and tell me exactly what the doctor said. Are they concerned about Daniel's asthma?"

Rita swallowed before replying. As she repeated the doctor's words, the situation didn't sound quite as dramatic as her behaviour suggested, "The doctor said not to worry. It's just a precaution because of his asthma and his age. Because of the shock of the bomb."

"I think the doctor is right. There is nothing to worry about," He looked at Daniel who had fallen asleep, "His breathing already seems a lot better, and I think he will be fine. You need some rest too, Rita. It has been a very tiring and stressful day for all of us. If you sit in a chair all night, you won't be able to sleep, and you will feel much worse tomorrow."

He released his hold on her hands and gently stroked her upper arm, "Come back to Julie and Vinny's with me, and we will feel much better when we see Daniel tomorrow."

Yansis was putting forward a very persuasive argument. If she was honest with herself, the events of the day had got to her, and she felt tense. He was right: spending all night in a hospital chair would only make her feel worse, and that wouldn't do Daniel any good. She knew that she would do a much better job of looking after Daniel if she felt well herself.

Apart from a good night's sleep, what she also needed

right now was a good, stiff drink to calm her nerves. So, against her better judgement, she agreed with Yansis that they would leave Daniel in the hospital overnight.

"I want to settle him into the ward first though, and make sure he's still asleep when we leave him."

"Of course, I want that too," said Yansis.

By the time Daniel was allocated to a ward, it was late evening. Apart from a few murmurings, he stayed asleep while they transferred him into the hospital bed.

"That Calpol they gave him must have done the trick," said Rita. "He's still flat out."

They both smiled fondly at Daniel before kissing him on the cheek and leaving the hospital.

Chapter 8

Manchester Daily Herald (evening edition)
Bomb Rips through City Centre

A huge bomb tore through the city centre this morning, injuring over 200 people.

The enormous blast occurred at approximately 11:20 from a device believed to have been planted in a van. The vehicle was parked outside the Arndale shopping centre on Corporation Street, directly across the road from Marks and Spencer.

Police believe the bomb to have been the work of the IRA following a telephone warning to a local television station at 10:00. The caller used a recognised IRA code word.

This is the second largest IRA attack on the British mainland, and the seventh IRA attack since the group broke its ceasefire in February.

After receiving the warning, police set up a cordon 400 metres around the suspect van. Police and other emergency services cleared the immediate vicinity of thousands of shoppers.

Army bomb disposal experts were called in to examine the van and carry out a controlled explosion. However, the bomb went off before they were able to do so.

Of the 200 plus injured, seven of them were serious, and a number of them were outside the cordoned area. Injuries were sustained as a result of debris and flying glass.

Many of the injured were taken to hospital by ambulance. Those with less serious injuries walked to one of three hospitals, which were on standby to receive the injured.

Among the first casualties to arrive at Manchester General Hospital were Rita Christos, Yansis Christos, Daniel Christos …

***

Raeni stared at the newspaper print, the names registering in her memory. Rita Christos, Yansis Christos and Daniel Christos. Although she didn't know the name of Rita's husband she knew he was Greek, and Christos certainly sounded Greek to her. She knew the name of her grandson though. His other grandmother, Joan, had told her when she made enquiries about him. It was Daniel.

She was convinced it must be them. It was too much of a coincidence not to be.

So, they were back in Manchester. And nobody even bothered to tell her. She put the newspaper to one side. She'd read enough for now. As devastating as the news was, she had her own sorrows to think about.

"What's wrong with you?" asked Jamal, on noticing her pained expression.

Raeni looked up at him through sad eyes, "My grandchild come home and nobody told me," she replied, the Jamaican patois becoming more pronounced in her agitation.

"What you on about?"

"Daniel, Leroy's boy. Who you think I'm on about? He's been in the bomb. Look, here! It's in the news," she said, thrusting the newspaper towards him.

"Well where is he now?"

"I don't know. I don't know where they're staying."

"Well you need to find out!" said Jamal, his anger rising. "He's your fuckin' grandkid. They've no right to keep him from you. He's my dead brother's kid too. That cheeky bitch had no right to take him over to Greece. It's about time someone taught her a fuckin' lesson."

"Alright, alright! No need for that language, boy. What have I told you about bad mouthing? I'm going round there now, see what his other grandmother can tell me."

Within a few minutes, Raeni walked the short distance to

Joan and Ged's house.

"Where are they?" asked Raeni when Joan answered the door.

"Who?"

"You know who. They back from the hospital yet?"

"What?"

"You don't know? About the bomb?"

"Course I know about the bomb. It's been on the news. But who are you talking about?"

"They been in the bomb in town. It's all over the papers. I know they been staying here. I seen their names in the paper. When your daughter comes back, you tell her I want to see my grandson. She got no right keeping him from me. She shouldn't have taken him out of the country in the first place. I'm his grandmother …"

"Oh my God! You mean Rita's been in the bomb? Is she OK? What about Daniel and Yansis?" Joan interrupted.

"Yes, they're alright. Check the paper. It's all in there. Minor injuries, it says. How long they been home anyway? And nobody bothered to tell me."

"I've got to go. I'll have to ring the hospital, see how they are," said Joan, and before Raeni could say anything more she shut the door firmly, leaving her standing on the other side.

***

Sunday 16th June 1996 - Morning
Despite Rita and Yansis's eagerness to fetch Daniel home, it was 9.30 a.m. before they arrived at hospital the following day. There was a heavy build-up of traffic heading towards the centre of Manchester. This delayed them as the hospital was on the outskirts of the city centre. Rita surmised that a

lot of the roads must still be blocked due to the aftermath of the bomb.

As they entered the corridor that led to the children's ward, they were greeted by the lovely nurse who had been so helpful to Rita the previous day. Rita was glad she could return her cheerful smile, now she was on her way to be reunited with her precious son.

"He's been absolutely fine," said the nurse. "His asthma's a lot better and he's been enjoying himself in the playroom this morning. He's a little angel, isn't he? You'll have to wait until the doctor does his rounds, but I think he'll probably discharge him today."

Rita swelled with pride as they continued to make their way towards the children's ward.

Her bonhomie didn't last long. As soon as they walked through the door she sensed there was something wrong. It was like a sixth sense. An ominous foreboding. '*Oh no. Please God, no!*' she thought.

"Where is he? His bed's empty?" she asked Yansis, the panic rising.

"Do not worry Rita. Remember, the nurse said he was in the playroom. That will be where he still is. Let's look."

Feeling momentarily reassured, she followed Yansis to the playroom but, as she had foreseen, he wasn't there. She knew. She just knew. It was something about this hospital. She knew something bad was going to happen. She had felt it and ignored her intuition.

"Where the hell is he?" she cried.

"Don't worry, Rita. We need to search properly, and ask all the nurses," said Yansis.

But Rita's intuition proved true. Despite them and the nurses scouring the entire ward and surrounding corridors, nobody found Daniel anywhere. By this time. Yansis had also lost his calm demeanour.

"Where can he be? I cannot believe he could walk out of a hospital and nobody would see him go."

"It's because they're not doing their bleedin' job properly! I said we shouldn't have left him," said Rita. "Heads will fuckin' roll over this. You mark my words."

Just at that moment, a senior hospital administrator appeared, and Rita vented her anger towards him while he tried to reassure them that the hospital staff were doing everything possible to find Daniel.

"We've issued an alert throughout the hospital and are checking all the exits. We've also called the police. They will need to speak to you when they arrive. Is there anything I can get for you in the meantime?"

"Not unless you can conjure up a five-year-old boy out of thin air," Rita replied sarcastically.

"Shussh, Rita. He is trying to help," Yansis cajoled. He turned to the hospital administrator. "Can you bring us both a cup of coffee please?" he asked.

When the administrator was gone, Rita said to Yansis, "I'm going out for a cig before the coppers get here. If they arrive before I've finished, they'll just have to bleedin' wait."

Rita was in turmoil. Between taking drags of her cigarette, she paced about outside the hospital. Desperate to catch a glimpse of Daniel. She peered through the windows into the corridors then watched people walk by. Young people. Old people. People with children. Boys. Girls. Teenagers. Toddlers.

But nobody looked like Daniel.

She rummaged inside her handbag, not sure what she was looking for. Something. Anything. To calm her shattered nerves.

She found it hard to believe. The two most precious

people in her life were Daniel and Yansis, and within the last twenty-four hours both of their lives had come under threat. Now her son was missing, and she couldn't handle it!

She was still seething with anger: her automatic coping mechanism. In desperation, she kicked at the wall to release some of her pent-up tension. But she wouldn't cry. She couldn't. She needed to hold it together. For all she knew her son might have just wandered off somewhere inside the hospital and could come back any minute. She tried telling herself that, but somehow she didn't believe it.

When Rita returned to the parents' waiting room where she had left Yansis, the police were already there. Two PCs introduced themselves. Rita had dealt with the police in the past and knew from experience that they weren't treating Daniel's disappearance seriously yet. Otherwise, they would have sent detectives rather than PCs. Nevertheless, they were keen to get down to business. The older of the two, a youngish man with dark hair, whose name had escaped Rita, was the keenest.

He began a series of questions, which Rita suspected he'd already asked Yansis. They were all standard, "What time did you arrive?" "Where did you check?" and so on, but Rita's patience was running out.

"Look, what's the point of going over this? Shouldn't you be searching near to the hospital, maybe setting up roadblocks or something? Whoever's got him could be bloody miles away by now!"

"Have you any reason to believe that somebody would have taken your son?" asked the PC.

Remembering her mother's call of the previous evening, when she told her about Raeni's visit, Rita felt she had no alternative but to inform the police. She explained the background of Daniel's parentage. Then she gave them details of the conversation with her mother, including Raeni's demands to see her grandson. The police asked for Raeni's address, and Rita asked them to wait a moment while she withdrew her Nokia phone from her handbag and rang her mother to ask for it.

One of the officers wrote it down, as well as the address where Rita and Yansis were staying. They then left the hospital after assuring Rita and Yansis that they would be in touch with them if they had anything to report.

By this time, Rita's anger had subsided, and she had entered a phase of regret and self-criticism.

"I bleedin' knew we shouldn't have left him here on his own," she said to Yansis. "Why didn't I listen to my instincts? I just knew something would go wrong. I can't believe I put my own needs before Daniel's."

"No, no! I can't let you think like that, Rita. It is not your fault," asserted Yansis. He stepped over to her, putting his arm around her shoulders in a reassuring gesture. "There is nothing else we can do here now. Let's go back to Julie and Vinny's, and wait to hear from the police. Hopefully they will have some good news for us soon."

Chapter 9

Daniel was standing outside the hospital looking for his parents.

"Where are mummy and daddy?" he asked the man who was holding on tight to his hand.

The man had told him they would be there waiting, and Daniel believed him. "Change into these clothes so your mam and dad can take you home," he said when he led him into the toilets while the hospital staff were occupied elsewhere. "Your parents are just parking the car," he had said. "They've sent me to fetch you. They've got a present for you, because you've been so brave."

Daniel believed every word. Despite warnings not to go off with strangers, the lure of a 'present' was too much.

"What's your favourite toy?" asked the man when he had engaged him in conversation inside the hospital.

"Thomas the Tank," Daniel replied, recalling the video he had watched with Julie's son the previous day.

"I think your mam and dad must have known that," said the man. "They've got you a Thomas the Tank train set in the car. But don't tell them I told you. It's supposed to be a surprise."

Daniel remembered the surprise his mother talked about yesterday. It added credence to the stranger's words, and a five-year-old didn't take much convincing. A Thomas the Tank train set! He couldn't wait to show it to Thomas.

As they waited outside the hospital, a vehicle approached.

"They're here now. Come on," said the man, pulling Daniel towards the car.

The driver brought the vehicle to a stop, and the man opened the rear passenger door. Daniel could see that there was a woman driving, but it wasn't his mummy. The man pushed him inside before he could protest, and the car sped off.

Daniel was confused, and he forgot all about the toy he had been promised. "Where are mummy and daddy?" he asked.

The man ignored him as he issued instructions to the female driver. At the same time he pinned him down to the seat, "Keep quiet and do as you're told, and you won't get hurt," he said.

His voice had taken on a different tone. It was now menacing rather than chatty. This swift change unnerved Daniel. He became frightened, sensing that something wasn't right. The tears sprang to his eyes, and he began to murmur.

"Shut it!" shouted the man. "I told you to keep quiet."

His booming tone was enough to quell Daniel's cries. He wept silent tears until the car drew to an abrupt halt a few streets from the hospital. The man chose a secluded side road. As soon as the vehicle stopped, he pulled Daniel out, and walked him round to the boot. He lifted the door. Inside were a roll of tape and some rope.

"Get in!" he ordered.

The thought of getting inside was so frightening to Daniel that he started crying uncontrollably. The man forced a hand over his mouth to silence him while he grasped hold of him with his other hand.

"Quick, get the tape on him," he instructed.

With the help of the woman, they soon covered Daniel's mouth, and bound his hands and feet. Daniel struggled as they threw him roughly into the boot. Once inside, they shut the door, and Daniel was seized by panic as he found himself in a dark, confined space.

Daniel felt the car start up again, and he was shunted about as it accelerated. He was lying awkwardly so his sore arm rubbed against the bottom of the boot. The pain on movement added to his distress.

It was a traumatic journey for a five-year-old: a journey of pain, darkness and fear. He felt abandoned. Where were his parents? He wanted them to help him. To take the pain and fear away. But he didn't know where they were.

When they reached their destination, the man opened the boot. Daniel was relieved that it was no longer dark, but scared of what would happen next. The man bent over him while he was still lying inside.

"Right, I'm gonna take the tape off, but no screaming, or else!"

The man glared at him angrily, and Daniel nodded in agreement. Daniel winced when he pulled the tape away as it tore the skin from his lips, and stung. His eyes filled with renewed tears and he was about to cry out, but the man flashed him a warning look.

Once the man had removed all of Daniel's ties, he instructed him to stand, and led him by the hand. Daniel noticed that the plaster that was covering the worst of his wounds was now loose. He became anxious as he knew that you must keep the dressing on if you had a sore.

The sight of blood seeping through the plaster added to his alarm, and he wanted to cry again. His arm was hurting him, and he needed another plaster. Mummy and daddy would have given him one. But he daren't ask. The man would only shout at him. Daniel was slowly realising that they weren't very nice people, and he was petrified.

***

Sunday 16th June 1996 - Afternoon

It was mid-afternoon and several hours since Daniel had disappeared. In the early stages of Daniel's disappearance, Rita and Yansis were still in a state of shock and hadn't fully absorbed the facts. At that point, there were many possibilities as to what might have happened.

As time moved on, however, they were becoming more convinced that something bad had taken place. They were both finding this difficult to accept.

Vinny had taken the children out to the park but Julie insisted on staying with Rita to give her and Yansis some support. In a way, Rita wished Julie had gone with him. It wasn't as if she could do anything to help.

Julie tried to offer reassurance. "He'll be fine. He's probably just wandered off and got lost somewhere near the hospital. I bet he'll turn up as right as rain."

But Rita was becoming irritated with the same tired clichés.

"What if he's not alright, though, Julie?" she asked. "What if something bad has happened to him?"

"Rita, you can't afford to think like that. Anything could have happened. It's still early; try to stay positive."

"It's not early though, is it? He's been gone for bloody hours!"

As they awaited news from the police, Rita was becoming increasingly agitated and couldn't settle. She was sitting next to Julie, picking at her nail varnish. She hovered on the edge of her seat, her shoulders hunched and head bowed. A tight knot had formed inside her stomach.

"I still can't understand how he could have got past the nursing staff?" she said for the umpteenth time. "Where can he have got to, for God's sake? I bet the poor little bugger's terrified!"

"He might not be, Rita. He might not even realise he's lost yet. He might think it's just a little adventure," said Julie, covering Rita's hand with hers.

"I'm worried about his asthma," said Yansis. "And those cuts. That one on his arm is really big."

The girls looked at Yansis who was standing next to the window where he had been watching the street for some time. When nobody responded to his comment, he continued looking for activity outside.

Several minutes passed in silence. Then Yansis suddenly leaned forward, observing the street more keenly. His swift movement startled Rita, who was already tense.

"What? What is it?" she asked.

"Nothing. It was just a car. I think it is going next door," said Yansis.

"For God's sake! Will you sit down?" she shouted, running her hands through her hair in her usual manner when under stress. "You've got me all on bleedin' edge!"

"I'm waiting for the police, Rita. You're not the only one who feels bad. He's my son too!"

She was ready to snap and knew it was wrong to take her despair out on him, so she went outside, taking her cigarettes with her. A few minutes later she was back, still anxious but able to keep her rising temper under wraps for the time being. She plonked herself on the sofa but couldn't settle. Her shoulders remained hunched and her back felt stiff.

They sat without speaking until the shrill ringing of the phone pierced the silence. Rita jumped, clutching her hand to her chest.

"Oh my God!" she said.

"It's OK," said Julie. "I'll answer it."

As Julie rushed to get the call, Rita shouted, "If it's my mam and dad, tell them I'm in the bathroom. I can't cope with them mithering at the moment."

After a few seconds, she followed Julie into the hallway, ready to take the receiver from her. She strained to overhear the conversation, but it sounded like it might be Julie's mother.

While Rita's focus was on Julie's phone call, Yansis announced, "A car has just stopped outside."

Rita rushed to join Yansis at the window. She established that it wasn't a police car, and was about to sit down again when she noticed two well-dressed young men get out of the car and walk up the garden path. Plain clothes. '*Oh my God! Now the police* are *taking it seriously*,' she thought.

"I'll get the door," shouted Julie, terminating her call when she heard the doorbell ring.

Rita sat back on the settee and was joined by Yansis as they mentally prepared themselves for news of their son.

The men walked into the room with an air of authority, especially the older of the two. He was a handsome man in his late thirties and, under normal circumstances, would have proved a welcoming distraction on a Sunday afternoon. As things stood though, his presence was inauspicious.

"Good afternoon, Mr and Mrs Christos. I am DI Collins and this is my colleague DS Fletcher." He indicated a younger man, thin and studious-looking. DI Collins proffered his hand towards Yansis, and Yansis and Rita quickly stood up in response to his greeting.

Rita remembered a previous occasion when she had dealings with the police. It had sparked in her a profound mistrust in them but she tried not to let it show. On first appearances this DI seemed to be a different character to the one she dealt with in the past when she and Julie ran into some trouble years ago.

"Please take a seat," said Julie, pointing towards the other sofa on the adjacent side of the room. "I'll get us all a drink. What would you like?"

The policemen and Yansis requested their drinks, and Rita automatically followed suit, even though it was one of many she had already consumed that day.

"Right," said DI Collins, once he was seated. "I want to start first of all by saying that I appreciate this is a difficult time for you both, and we are doing everything we can to find your son. Our officers are currently checking the CCTV systems at the hospital, and have been interviewing the staff and any other people who were present around the time of your son's disappearance. We will be following up any leads and will notify you as soon as we know anything."

Rita felt a lump in her throat on hearing these words. She now realised that they definitely were taking Daniel's disappearance very seriously, and the impact of this realisation stunned her. Yansis took hold of her hand, and she fought to maintain control of her emotions.

"C-can you tell us anything yet?" she asked even though she knew it was a pointless question. The DI had already said they'd tell them once they knew anything.

"Not yet, but I can assure you that we are trying to gather as much information as possible. We've just come back from visiting Mrs Samuels …"

The DI paused on seeing the look of confusion on Rita and Yansis's faces.

"Your son's grandmother," he elaborated.

"Oh, Raeni," said Rita, who hadn't known Raeni's surname and didn't realise that it was different from Leroy's.

"Yes, Raeni Samuels. I believe her deceased son, Leroy Booth, was the child's father."

"His natural father, yes, but we adopted him and have brought him up since he was a baby."

"I see."

Just that moment, Julie walked in carrying a tray of drinks, and interrupted the discussion.

"I'll make myself scarce, shall I?" she asked once she'd given the drinks out.

"No, it's OK," said Rita. "Stay here."

"Right, as I was saying," continued DI Collins. "We've just returned from speaking to Mrs Samuels. We questioned her about Daniel's disappearance, and I can confirm that there is no evidence to suggest that she has the child. In fact, she was quite distraught by the fact that Daniel had disappeared."

"Are you sure?" asked Rita, "Only, according to my mam, she was kicking up a right fuss because we hadn't been to see her. And apparently, she's been asking to see him for the last five years."

"I'm afraid that isn't a crime in itself. We took a look around Mrs Samuels' home, and found no signs of a small child being kept there." Before Rita could cut in, he continued. "Now, we would like to go over some questions with you. I appreciate that you have already spoken to two of our PCs this morning but we would like to go through everything with you again. Can you tell me at what point you realised that your son was missing?"

Rita felt herself becoming tetchy but she knew that they were just doing their job. Something about the DI's manner suggested that he was efficient and had their best interests at heart. In fact, he was dispelling her previous perceptions of the police so she cooperated in the hope that it would help.

The two officers asked Rita and Yansis numerous questions, many of which they'd already answered that morning. When the questioning was drawing to a close, the DI hit them with, "Is there anything else you can think of that may help us with our enquiries, anything at all?"

Rita felt Julie's eyes focus on her from across the room, and knew that she was thinking of her venomous Aunty Irene and what she said at the wedding. She gave Julie a warning look in response, and was relieved that Yansis and the officers didn't pick up on it.

"No, there's nothing," Rita replied before Julie and Yansis had a chance to speak.

"Right, well that will be all for today," the DI concluded.

The two officers crossed the room and shook their hands again, before Julie led them to the front door. Just before he left, DI Collins turned round. "We'll be in touch as soon as we know anything," he repeated.

When Julie came back into the living room, she asked Rita, "Why didn't you mention that aunty of yours and the way she carried on at the wedding? It could be relevant."

"No, it won't be her. Don't be daft," said Rita, hastily. "She might be a nasty old cow but she wouldn't do Daniel any harm. If I go telling the police what she said, it will only cause a load of trouble in the family, and we've had more than enough trouble over the years."

Julie didn't look convinced but that wasn't Rita's concern. At least she had stopped her from getting the police involved where they weren't wanted.

For a few minutes they stayed in the living room, analysing what the officers had said, and desperately trying to draw conclusions. But they were going around in circles, and weren't getting anywhere.

"I'm still not convinced about Raeni," said Rita. "She's the likeliest suspect if you ask me. It sounds like they've let her off too easily. Just because Daniel's not at her house, doesn't mean she hasn't got him parked up with one of her relatives or friends. I think we need to find out for ourselves."

"Oh no!" Yansis and Julie both said at once.

Rita's impulsiveness and strength of character had got them into trouble in the past so they were both anxious to stop her going. Rita, however, had other ideas.

"Look, I can't stand all this waiting. We need to do something. Sitting around here is driving me up the bleedin' wall! I'm going to see her and you can please yourself, Yansis. But if you don't come with me, you know I'll go anyway, with or without you."

When Rita saw the look on his face, she knew she'd won the argument. Yansis's passivity was never a match for Rita's forcefulness.

Chapter 10

Monday 17th June 1996

Rita approached the house with trepidation. Although it was her idea to visit Leroy's mother, she was now having second thoughts. She didn't even know the woman. All she knew about her were the impressions she'd gained through her son, Leroy, and her own mother. Rita wasn't encouraged by the fact that Raeni had brought Leroy into the world but, according to her mam, Raeni wasn't a bad sort.

Rita realised she'd have to take the lead; Yansis hadn't wanted to come in the first place. He only came to prevent her from getting into any bother, and perhaps because there was a part of him that thought they might get a little nearer to finding out where Daniel was.

An overweight, middle-aged, black woman answered the door, and she didn't give a very warm reception. Rita assumed she must be Raeni.

"What do you want?" she snapped.

"I-I'm Rita. This is my husband, Yansis. We wondered if we could talk to you."

"I've got nothing to say. I said all I had to say to those policemen. Coming here, asking their questions. I suppose you think I've got the boy too, do you?"

"No, no, it's not that. It's just that I wondered if you might know anything that might help."

"And why would I know anything?"

Rita could feel the hostility emanating from Raeni who didn't show any signs of wanting a reasoned discussion.

"Look, I'm sorry but we're desperate. I don't know what we'll do if we don't get him back," said Rita, her voice shaking. "If there's anything at all that will help us find him, please tell us."

Raeni paused for a moment, and Rita thought she detected a slight softening of her features, but then her hostility turned to annoyance.

"I can't believe your cheek, woman! Five years, *five years* you been away, and I haven't seen my grandson once in all that time. Now, as soon as there's anything wrong, you come running round here with your accusations."

Despite Rita's initial reservations, she could match anyone for temper, and her lack of progress prompted an equally irate response.

"Hang on a minute, we haven't accused anybody! We're just asking if you can help, that's all. Do you really think we'd be round here if we weren't desperate? If you had any sense of decency you'd realise what we're going through and try to help us!"

"You think I don't know? You think I'm not upset? I know how it feels to lose a son, and now I might have lost my grandson too. And I never even got to see him!"

Raeni's angry words acted like a shock wave that shot through Rita, and stunned her into silence. For a few moments the two women stood glaring furiously at each other, the atmosphere between them like electricity.

It seemed to bring Raeni to her senses too because she looked beyond Rita and Yansis, as though aware that their raised voices might attract attention. Then she appeared to relent as she said, "You'd better come inside."

"Sit down," ordered Raeni when they were indoors.

They did as they were told but, now they were inside, Rita was determined to put her point across.

"I'm sorry if I was a bit insensitive," she said. "I didn't want Daniel on the Riverhill Estate; not after what happened to Jenny."

"You're talking rubbish, woman! Just because of what happened to your sister, doesn't mean the same will happen to Daniel. He'd only be visiting; he doesn't have to live here. Not like my sons. We all still have to live here. You're lucky you've got a choice."

"Well, I don't feel very lucky at the moment," said Rita.

Despite Raeni's anger, Rita could sense the conflict that was taking place within her: concern for Daniel's current welfare was battling with her fury over not seeing him. Rita guessed that there was a caring woman behind the stern exterior, and she capitalised on that. "Look, Daniel has asthma. Quite bad. He has to take his inhalers regularly or he'll get really ill. The longer he's away, the more ill he'll become."

"I know all about asthma," said Raeni, who was now becoming calmer. "I've had it myself for years."

"He's got some injuries from the bomb blast too. He's had stitches, but they could still get infected if he doesn't have his dressings changed regularly."

Raeni nodded at Rita, so she continued, "We took Daniel to Greece because we thought it was the best thing for him. He has a good life there. We can give him all the things that he wouldn't have if he stayed here. I don't want him to end up like Jenny, and I'm sure you …"

"Enough!" said Raeni, stopping Rita before she mentioned Leroy's death. Raeni then remained quietly observing them until Rita broke the silence.

"I'll leave you my mobile number," she said. "If you do find out anything, please will you let us know as soon as possible?"

She took a pen out of her bag, tore the top off a cigarette packet and scribbled her number on it. As she passed the piece of card to Raeni, she noticed her sorrow-filled expression.

Raeni then led them out of the house without saying anything further.

***

Monday 17th June 1996

"I lot of bleedin' help you were," Rita said to Yansis once they were outdoors.

"Rita, you forget that I didn't want to go to the house. It was your idea. I think she is a very sad and lonely lady, and there is no point making her feel worse. Besides, I don't think she has Daniel."

"OK, OK, big bad Rita strikes again, I get it … Right, well now we're here, we might as well go round and see my mam and dad."

"Oh no, Rita. I hope you are not going to tell them what your aunty said at the wedding."

"Why not? Someone has to face them with it. They must have been having a moan to her, otherwise where did she get her ideas from? Besides, they've got off easily. I could have told the police about Aunty Irene but I didn't. Anyway, I'll tread carefully. It's not as if I'm gonna accuse them or anything."

Yansis looked at her and raised his eyebrows. Subtlety wasn't always her strong point, and her relationship with her father had been unstable for a long time.

"Look, Yansis. Do we want our son back or don't we?"

"Of course I want Daniel back."

Rita knew she had him. "In that case," she said, "we need to do whatever it takes."

A few minutes later they were inside Rita's parents'

home, which was only a few streets away from Raeni's, on the Riverhill Estate.

Initially they received a much more sympathetic reception than they had done at Raeni's, and both her parents were full of concern about Daniel.

"Any news yet, love?" asked her mother, Joan.

Rita briefly covered the visit they had received from the two police officers that afternoon, adding. "I suppose they must be taking it seriously if they've sent detectives."

"Well try not to worry, love. I'm sure they'll come back to you with some news soon."

Rita didn't mention her visit to Raeni; instead she wanted to focus on the subject she was about to raise. Aunty Irene.

"Aunty Irene had a word with me at the wedding," she began. Then, when she had the rapt attention of both her parents, she continued. "She was a bit accusing, telling me I'd really upset you both when I took Daniel to live in Greece."

"Oh, you know what Aunty Irene's like. You don't want to take any bloody notice," said Joan.

"Yeah but, it's not easy when she's in my face. She insinuated that you were both against us taking Daniel to Greece so I told her that wasn't the impression I had."

"We never said that!" snapped Ged.

"Well where has she got the idea from, then?"

"I don't bloody know, do I? Anyway, why you bringing it up now?"

"No reason. I just wondered what would make her think that you didn't want us to take Daniel to Greece. She seemed to think you were really upset about it."

"What are you trying to imply?" said Ged. "I hope you're not saying that my family have got anything to do with Daniel disappearing."

"No, course I'm not. But she was really nasty to me."

"That's just her way," said Ged. "I'll have a word with her, tell her to keep her nose out. But I hope you've not gone and said anything to the police. I'll be really pissed off if you have. The last thing we need is them sniffing round."

"No, course I haven't."

While Rita questioned her parents, she observed them for any signs they might be lying. Changes in their tone. Fidgeting. Rushing to get their words out. Her father's voice had risen and speeded up but that was usual when he was hassled. That could just be because he was worried she'd mentioned it to the police. So there was really no way of knowing, and she decided not to push things further.

Deep down, though, she didn't really suspect her parents of snatching Daniel. Despite her negative opinion of her father, she doubted whether even he would do something so callous. But she had to be sure.

Her aunty, on the other hand, was an unknown quantity, and Rita didn't know her so well. Although she didn't like to think that someone in her own family could have done her son harm, her aunty's attitude at the wedding had raised her suspicions.

As they made their way to Julie's, Yansis asked, "Well, are you happy now?"

"Yansis, I won't be happy until we get Daniel back. But if you mean am I satisfied now that I've seen Raeni and my parents, the answer's 'no'. I don't think we're any further forward."

"Surely you can't think your parents are connected with Daniel's disappearance?"

"Not really, but I wouldn't trust Aunty Irene as far as I could throw her."

"But why would she want Daniel?"

"I don't know. She probably wouldn't want him for herself. Maybe in some warped way she might think she was doing my mam and dad a favour."

Yansis didn't respond but the expression on his face showed his scepticism.

"I know, it sounds crazy, but weirder things have happened. And I was thinking of all the cases of missing kids you see in the news. Nine times out of ten the family are involved ... Oh, don't worry, I don't think my mam and dad are. I think I would have been able to tell if there was anything suspicious going on. I'm sorry Yansis, you must think I'm terrible, but I just needed to make sure."

"It's OK, Rita, I understand," he said, taking her hand. "I want Daniel back too."

"I suppose all we can do now is wait for the police to get in touch again," she said.

Chapter 11

Monday 17th June 1996

"Alright, mate?" asked Tony when John arrived at work.

"So, so," he replied.

"Why, what's up?"

John told Tony about Daniel going missing, which elicited an impassioned response from him.

"Jesus, I didn't realise it was your nephew! It's the talk of the station. Well, that and the bomb."

"I bet it is. Well, do me a favour, Tony, and keep it to yourself, will you? I can do without a load of well-wishers reminding me about it every five minutes."

"Sure; whatever you say, mate."

"What have we got lined up today, anyway?"

"Not sure yet, but I think it might be something connected with the bomb. It's a pity 'cos I think we're chasing shadows there. We've got no chance of putting those bastards behind bars. I wish we were going out on another raid instead. That one at Harpurhey last week went brilliantly. I still can't believe how easy it was."

"Yeah, it was a good shout," was John's lacklustre response.

"You alright mate?"

John shrugged his shoulders.

"I'm not surprised it's getting to you. I'd be climbing the fuckin' walls, and wanting to have the bastard's balls on a plate."

"I think you're jumping the gun a bit," John snapped. "We don't know if someone's got him yet."

"No, I know, but he's been missing since yesterday, hasn't

he? You know how these things go mate … Look, I'm sorry. I'm not trying to wind you up or anything. I'm just stating the facts."

Tony then paused and John felt as though he was psyching himself up to add something more. His suspicions proved correct when Tony said, "You could use your inside influence if you wanted to. I think I would. In fact, I know I would. If it was one of my family, I'd have to get involved."

"You know as well as I do that I can't tamper with a case. I'd be well in the shit."

"Oh, I know about the protocol and all that. It's different when it's your own family though, isn't it? Anyway, I'm just saying what I'd do. It's your choice at the end of the day."

"DI Collins is a good cop. I'm sure he's covering all the bases," said John, but his statement lacked conviction.

It wasn't as if he hadn't been tempted to see what he could find out. Thoughts of what could have happened to his nephew were driving him crazy. Aside from the fact that he was missing, it was the utter impotence at being unable to do anything about it.

Up to now his sense of duty had stopped him from acting against protocol. Besides, as far as he knew, the investigating officers didn't yet have much to go on anyway. It would be easy to find out how much information they did have. His ex-girlfriend, Janet, was on DI Collins' team, and she was still sweet on him. He could work that to his advantage. But he wouldn't. It wouldn't be fair to place her in an awkward position.

***

Monday 17th June 1996

Maurice put down his heavy bags. He was starting to find

his way around the local shopping areas, and had found some bargains in Quality Save and the pound shops. The house was coming together. It wasn't a palace; nothing matched and his purchases were more practical than aesthetic, but it suited his needs.

The bits that he bought would come in handy, and he was looking forward to putting them all in their place. It was still only morning so he had plenty of time to sort things out. Before he made a start, he decided to have a drink and a sit down. He'd no sooner taken off his shoes and switched on the kettle than he heard a knock on the front door.

He knew who they were as soon as he saw them, despite the absence of uniform. Police. He'd been expecting them. Whenever a child went missing, the local paedophiles were always the first port of call. Maurice had experienced several dealings with the police last time he was released from prison.

"Come in," he said, resigned to their presence and hoping none of the neighbours would figure out the connection.

The policemen got straight down to business. "I'm DI Collins, and this is DS Fletcher," said the older of the two. "We're here in connection with a missing child."

"I know," said Maurice.

DI Collins raised his eyebrows, "What do you mean?"

"I heard about the child. Daniel Christos, isn't it? I knew you'd be round sooner or later." Maurice's voice was monotone and lacked expression.

The policemen looked at him in eager anticipation. Maurice was enjoying toying with them. He couldn't help himself. "I'm the local paedo, aren't I? I suppose you'll be here every time a child goes missing."

"It looks like we've got a smart Alec here," said DS Fletcher but it was the DI who was becoming inflamed.

"Look, you piece of shit!" he said. "You can quit feeling sorry for yourself. Have you any idea what that child's family are going through?"

Maurice shrugged.

"Right, we're taking you in for questioning," continued the DI.

"What?" protested Maurice. "I haven't done anything."

"We can decide that once you've answered our questions."

DI Collins nodded at the sergeant who took Maurice's arm and led him towards the front door. "Have you got your keys?" he asked.

"Yes," said Maurice, who still had them in his pocket.

"Well, in that case, let's not waste any time."

Once he was at the station, and the police had booked him in, they left him in an interview room for a while.

Maurice waited patiently. He'd been through all this before and knew they'd come when they were ready. Sure enough, after a while DI Collins entered followed by DS Fletcher. The sergeant announced that the interview was to commence, and flicked the switch on the recorder.

"Right, let's get straight to the point, shall we?" said the inspector. "Can you tell me what you were doing outside the paediatrics department of Manchester General Hospital yesterday morning, Sunday the 16th of June 1996?"

The question floored Maurice. He had expected the usual standard questions relating to his whereabouts when the child disappeared and so on. He hadn't anticipated that they would have placed him at the hospital. CCTV! He should have known. The bloody things were everywhere these days.

He recalled his fascination with a case a few years ago when a child was snatched from a shopping centre in Liverpool. Police had spotted two youths taking him away through a check of the CCTV. Maurice watched the news coverage in prison. Since then, the use of CCTV had become increasingly widespread. Despite realising this, he responded on impulse with a rapid denial.

But there was no disputing the police evidence that placed him at the scene, so eventually there was nothing he could do but admit that he was there.

"Right," continued the DI. "So now we've established that you were at the hospital, perhaps you could tell us what you were doing there?"

"Just watching."

The DI exchanged a look of concern with DS Fletcher who asked, "What were you watching?"

"The children," whispered Maurice.

"Why?" asked the sergeant.

Maurice remained silent.

"I asked why!"

Still no reply.

DI Collins consulted a file in front of him. "According to your prison records, you attended a programme to help rehabilitate you into society. Is that right?" he asked.

"Yes."

"Is it wise to be watching children knowing the temptations that will bring?"

Again Maurice remained silent.

"What time did you arrive at the hospital and how long were you there?"

Maurice gave sketchy details of the approximate times of his arrival and departure.

"How come you know the child's name?" asked DI Collins.

The questions continued for a while until Maurice allowed a break. Then the interrogation resumed with the two officers going over the same questions, but reworded slightly in an attempt to catch him out.

Despite hours of skilled questioning, the suspect gave nothing away.

Chapter 12

Tuesday 18th June 1996

Irene gave the ornaments on the fireplace a quick dust then put them back in place. Each one stood in its exact location, strategically placed like a sentry on duty.

"Irene, for God's sake, will you sit down?" said Ged. "We've come to talk to you, not to see how tidy your bloody house is."

She walked over to her armchair and sat down, pulling her skirt straight beneath her and smoothing down the front of it to minimise creasing. Her whole demeanour suggested she was uncomfortable with this visit.

Joan watched her removing imaginary specks of dust from the arms of her chair, and plucking small bobbles from her twinset. On the rare occasions when Joan had met Irene, she was usually wearing a Marks and Spencer tweed skirt with matching blouse and smart cardigan or a knitted twinset. She rarely removed her cardigan, even in the summer months. Joan supposed it was because she was a doctor's receptionist and was used to keeping up appearances.

Joan willed Ged to get it over with. She still found it hard to believe at times that this was Ged's sister: they were so different. Irene was a bit of a snob whereas Ged was just the opposite.

"Well, what is it you want to talk to me about?" she asked after waiting a few moments for Ged to speak.

"It's our Daniel, he's gone missing."

"Really? Well well, that's a turn-up."

"You might at least act like you're sorry."

"I've got nothing to feel sorry about, Ged. But if you mean, do I care? Then of course I do. He's only a young child, and a member of this family. What exactly has happened?"

Ged and Joan described the events leading up to Daniel's disappearance. On realising the seriousness of the situation, and perhaps to make up for her cold initial response, Irene muttered some words of concern. Then Ged said, "Course, I know you didn't approve of our Rita taking the lad to Greece."

"I only said what needed saying. It's not right keeping a child from its grandparents. It must have been heartbreaking for you, especially after that other business with Jenny. I'm surprised you let her take him. That's your trouble, Ged, you've always been too … casual about things."

Irene's criticism provoked a reaction from Ged. "What d'you mean by that?" he asked.

"You know what I mean, Ged. You should take more responsibility. I suppose you're still spending most of your time in the pub, are you?"

"What the hell's it got to do with you if I am? What I do with my life is my own business. You should learn to keep your nose out instead of stirring things up with our Rita. What would you know about kids anyway? You haven't bleedin' got any of your own."

"There's no need to take that tone with me, Ged."

"Well, get off my case then."

"Alright, but I just wondered how you both felt about her taking the child to Greece."

"It's beside the point now, isn't it?" asked Ged, trying to deflect from the topic.

"What about you, Joan?" asked Irene.

Joan felt uncomfortable at being put on the spot. "I wasn't

completely happy," she murmured. "But like Ged says, it's beside the point now," she added, with a tremor in her voice.

It was something she had never previously admitted. She had just gone along with everybody else's wishes, knowing it would have cramped Ged's style to bring up another child at their age, and that Daniel would have a better life with Rita and Yansis.

Apart from that, it was Jenny's wish. And that hurt. Joan had private moments over the years when she'd cried over the daughter she'd lost and the grandchild she hardly ever saw, but she preferred to keep her feelings to herself. Now, forced to think about the situation, the tears flooded into her eyes and she felt embarrassed in front of Ged's sister.

Irene puffed up her chest, pursed her lips and looked down her nose in a self-satisfied manner. "That proves my point," she said. "I was right to say something at the wedding. Rita had no right to …"

"Turn it in will you? Can't you see she's upset?" interrupted Ged.

They remained silent for several minutes until Irene broke the tension, "Look, I understand you're a bit upset about the child," she said, as though only just realising that her self-righteous preaching was inappropriate under the circumstances.

Hearing her attempts at mollification, Ged seized the opportunity, "Aye, but you wouldn't have taken the lad, would you?" he asked.

"Of course not! What do you take me for?"

Turning to Joan, Ged said, "There, what did I tell you?" This question was guaranteed to drive a wedge between his sister and his wife, whether asked unwittingly or otherwise. Realising this, Joan stared back at him, too astonished to respond.

By the time they left Irene's home, brother and sister were on relatively amicable terms again. It was Joan who witnessed his true feelings on the matter once they got outside.

"What the bloody hell was wrong with you, getting all upset and showing us up like that? I thought we'd all agreed at the time that it was best if the kid went to live with Rita. Then you go and make it look as if we were bloody cheating you out of him or summat."

"I can't help getting upset, Ged. He's our grandson and he's missing. We're no further forward than before we came."

"Ha, that's where you're wrong. At least we know that stuck up cow hasn't got him."

"Yeah, if you believe her."

"Well, I don't think she's lying anyway. I had a quick scout round upstairs when I went for a piss. There's no way she's got him in the house, you mark my words."

Chapter 13

Tuesday 18ᵗʰ June 1996 - Afternoon

"Are you alright, Rita?" asked Julie for the umpteenth time that day. Her sympathy was getting on Rita's nerves. Everything was getting on Rita's nerves. She just wanted Daniel back, and she couldn't settle until she caught sight of his lovely little face.

The phone rang in the hall and Julie went to answer it before Rita had a chance. "I'm not here unless it's the police with some news," Rita shouted to Julie's retreating back, but she wasn't sure whether she heard.

"It's your mam," said Julie, a few seconds later.

"That's all I bloody need," Rita muttered to herself.

Guessing that Julie had already told her mother she was there, Rita went to take the call.

"Hello, Rita, is that you?" asked Joan.

"Yeah."

"Jesus, Rita! You'll never guess what."

"What?" asked Rita, becoming impatient.

"It's in the paper about our Daniel. The police have got a man."

"You what?"

"It's true! They've got someone in for questioning."

"You're joking!"

Yansis rushed into the hall on hearing Rita's reaction.

"What is it Rita? What has happened?"

Rita turned her face away from the phone while she addressed Yansis. "It's my mam. She says it's in the paper … the police have got someone." Before Yansis could respond, she spoke into the receiver again. "What did they say,

Mam?"

There was a catch in Joan's voice as she spoke, "Oh Rita, you're not gonna like this. He's one of them bleedin' paedophiles."

"Jesus Christ, no! Are you sure, Mam? Why haven't the police been in touch? What else does it say?"

"That's about it, love. It's only short. It just says they're holding a man for questioning in connection with the missing child, Daniel Christos, and that he's a known sex offender."

"Fuckin' hell, I don't believe it! Right Mam, I've got to go. I'm ringing the coppers *now*. I wanna know what's going on, and why they haven't bleedin' said owt!"

She put the receiver down without giving her mother a chance to say anything further.

"Yansis, have you got that DI's phone number?"

"Hang on a minute, Rita. Let us look at the newspaper first. You need to calm down before we speak to him."

"Oh, for fuck's sake. Julie!" she shouted. "Have you got the paper? I need to have a look."

Rita tore through the house looking for Julie who was no longer in the living room. She found her in her home office.

"Julie, have you got a newspaper? I need to check something."

Rita's rushed words and frantic behaviour took Julie by surprise. "Er, no. No, I haven't got one. What's the matter, Rita?"

"Some bastard paedo's got Daniel. I can't believe the fuckin' police haven't even bothered to tell us."

"We'll get a newspaper from the shop, Rita," said Yansis who had followed her through the house.

"No, I'm not fuckin' waiting. I'm ringing them *now*! I want to know what the bleedin' hell's going on with my son.

Where's his number?"

"No, Rita. I will ring. You're too upset," said Yansis.

But Rita wouldn't be dissuaded. She picked up her handbag and started rifling through its contents until she found what she was looking for: DI Collins's card. Marching through to the hall, she grabbed the phone, quickly dialled the number and demanded to speak to him.

After trying unsuccessfully to speak to DI Collins on the phone, Rita slammed it down and announced to Yansis and Julie, "The bastard's not available."

"OK, calm down, Rita," said Julie. "We'll get hold of him. I'll ring the station and ask them to get him to ring back once he's free. Or, I could ask for the sergeant if you like."

"No, I'll fuckin' get hold of him alright. Come on, Yansis. We're going down the station, and we're not leaving there until we find out what the hell's going on."

This was one occasion when Yansis didn't argue against Rita's impulsive nature. He was also anxious to get to the bottom of things.

By the time they arrived at the station, Rita had calmed down a little but she was still worried about her son's whereabouts. Thoughts of what might have happened to him had tormented her all the way there. As usual, Yansis was the voice of reason despite also being concerned about Daniel.

"Now remember what I said, Rita," he prompted, before they walked through the entrance. "If you start to shout it will make it more difficult for everybody. We will find out more if you try to stay calm."

"OK," she said, looking at him wistfully. "I'm sorry I went off on one. It's just …"

But she couldn't continue. Her emotions were threatening to overwhelm her and she swallowed down the lump in her throat.

"It's alright, Rita. I understand," said Yansis, taking her hand and leading her through the doors.

"I'm still not going home till we've seen him though," she added before they reached the reception desk.

They soon established that DI Collins was in the station but was tied up in interviews. Rita shuddered at the thought that he might be interviewing a child molester right at this moment. It might even be the man who had Daniel locked away somewhere.

She tried not to become agitated as she and Yansis explained the situation. The uniformed WPC seemed sympathetic and asked them to wait while she looked for somebody who could help. She also offered them a drink while they were waiting. Yansis was right. It was better to stay calm to enlist as much cooperation as possible.

They waited a long time, and Yansis was getting twitchy as well as Rita. When they were eventually led through to a sparse interview room, DI Collins stood up from behind a Formica-covered table. He shook each of their hands in turn then prompted them to sit down before doing the same himself.

"I imagine you've seen the press coverage." It was a statement rather than a question but Rita replied anyway.

"No, but we've heard about it. Why didn't you tell us? You said you'd be in touch as soon as you had any information."

"Because, at the moment, we don't have anything. The man is being questioned. He isn't under arrest."

"You must have had your reasons for bringing him in. I believe he's a known sex offender," said Rita, her voice trailing off as she said the last two words.

"Yes, which is why we would have preferred not to make

an announcement at this stage. There is no point causing you undue distress when we haven't any proof that the man has actually done anything."

"Why are you questioning him, then? Are you questioning all the paedos?" she asked.

DI Collins let out a sigh. "Not exactly, no. Although it's standard for us to look at anyone with a history of child sex offences in a case like this, we have ruled out a number of people on various grounds."

"But why are you holding this one?" asked Rita.

DI Collins paused before replying. "He was spotted … on the hospital premises. It was around the time your son went missing. The CCTV systems picked him up."

He held out his hand to prevent a response, but wasn't quick enough to stop Yansis from uttering, "Oh my God!"

"Please! Let's not jump to conclusions," said the inspector. "That is the only evidence we have at the moment. We have to cover all the bases but it might be totally unconnected to your son's disappearance. I promise, if he admits to anything or if any other evidence comes to light, we'll let you know."

"Why am I not convinced?" asked Rita, sarcastically. It was an attempt at bravado, to disguise her inner turmoil.

Realising that the DI wasn't going to offer anything more, Rita stood up to go. She needed to get outside. Yansis also stood up, but he spoke a few parting words to the DI, "We feel very let down. To find out through the press is wrong. You shouldn't have let that happen."

"I can only apologise," said DI Collins, but they left before he could say anything more.

Outside, Rita was beyond anger. Instead, she was full of sorrow and despair. When Yansis took her in his arms, she looked into his tear-filled eyes before nuzzling her head into his chest and releasing her emotions. It was several minutes before her sobbing subsided and she was calm enough to walk to the car.

It was hard to describe how she felt after their visit to the police station. Helpless? Inadequate? Ashamed? She didn't do helpless and inadequate; they weren't normally a part of her makeup. But ashamed somehow felt like the closest definition to suit her present feelings.

Not only had she let her sister down but she had let her son down too. And when she should have been fulminating against the injustice of it all, what did she do? She sat there speechless while DI Collins offered nothing but platitudes. Then, outside, she'd broken down, weak and helpless like a faded image of her former self.

Rita had been through a lot. She'd battled for years, refusing to become a victim of her circumstances. And she'd made a better life for herself; a happy life in Greece with her wonderful husband, Yansis, and the son that meant everything to them. And now their son had been snatched.

But she wouldn't, she COULDN'T, let it sink her. She had to pull herself together again and continue fighting. It was Rita's way of coping, and the only way she could get through this.

When they returned to Julie's, Rita filled her in on the details. Then, after one of Julie's many comforting cups of tea, the next thing Rita did was to ring her brother, John. She may have succumbed to her emotions for a short while, but she wasn't defeated yet.

"Have you heard the news?" she asked, when he answered the phone.

"Yeah, are you OK?"

"Not really. Me and Yansis have just been to see DI Collins but he wouldn't tell us bugger all. Why have they arrested this man? What have they got on him?"

"I've no idea, Rita."

"Well you're a copper, John. You must know summat."

"I don't get access to that information. It's only usually open to people who are working directly on the case. And, even if I did, I wouldn't be able to tell anyone what was going on. It's more than my job's worth."

"Aw come on. You must be able to find out something. There must be ways around it. Have you any idea what me and Yansis are going through? I would have thought your family were more important to you than your poxy job!"

"Look, Rita. I'd help you out if I could. You know I would, but I just can't."

Rita sighed down the phone before continuing. "Right, well if you can't tell me what they've got on him, can you tell me how the newspapers found out about it? Other coppers must have access to information if someone tipped off the papers."

"I don't know. It's probably not the police that tipped them off; it could be anything Reet. Maybe the security staff at the hospital knew the police were onto something. They might have even been instructed to notify the police if they saw the man hanging about the hospital again."

"What d'you mean, 'onto something'? That sounds like they do think it's him. Oh my God, John! If that man's done anything to harm Daniel, I swear, I'll kill the bastard with my own bare hands."

"You'll have to join the queue." Then, as if realising he had spoken out of turn for an officer of the law, he added. "Look, it might be nothing. They're just following procedure. They always check out all the local paedophiles when something like this happens, but it doesn't necessarily mean he's guilty."

"Why was he in the bloody hospital then?" asked Rita.

"I don't know, but if the police had enough on him they'd have made an arrest, and they haven't done, so try not to worry."

"That's easy for you to say. I'm tearing my bloody hair out here!"

"I know, I'm sorry, Rita. Like I say, if I could do anything, I would. He's my nephew too, don't forget."

Rita came off the phone, disheartened that she wasn't able to elicit any help from her brother, but determined that she would find a way to bring her son back.

Chapter 14

Tuesday 18th June 1996

"Did Jamal know about Daniel being kept in the hospital?" Raeni asked her younger son, Devan.

"I don't know. Why, what's wrong?"

"Them saying in the paper about this paedophile but I'm not so sure."

"What you trying to say?"

"There's something funny if you ask me. Why hasn't your brother been home since the child went missing?"

"Come off it, Mam. Our Jamal wouldn't do owt like that."

"Well, he was angry enough about them taking Daniel to Greece and not bringing him to see me. Matter of fact, that was one of the things he said the last time I seen him."

"So! That doesn't mean anything. He was right; they were out of order."

Raeni reached over from the chair where she was sitting and put her hand on Devan's shoulder, pleading with him. "Do you know where Jamal is, Devan? I haven't seen him since Sunday. I tried ringing that mobile phone he has, but he won't answer any of my calls."

Devan pulled away from her. "I don't know owt. Why you hassling me?"

"Because you're his brother." Raeni's voice began to crack as the emotion threatened to overwhelm her. "I know he tells you things. I need to know where he is, Devan. He's my son, and that missing child is my grandchild. If you see Jamal, please ask him to bring the child home safe."

"I've told you, I don't know anything. For fuck's sake!" Devan replied as he rose from the sofa and stormed out of the room.

"Well at least tell me where he hangs about then!" Raeni shouted to his retreating back, but she was wasting her time. She tutted to herself at his use of bad language, but was too troubled to pursue the matter. He wouldn't take any notice anyway. They never did.

Although Raeni was convinced that Devan knew something, he was refusing to tell her what it was. She'd keep trying though. It was too much of a coincidence that Jamal hadn't been home since around the time of Daniel's disappearance. Of course, she didn't tell the police any of this. She wanted to prevent her sons from getting into trouble if she could, and voicing her suspicions to the police would only make matters worse.

It wasn't the first time Jamal had spent days away from home. In fact, she was forever complaining that he used the place like a hotel. But something wasn't right. She could sense it, and she wouldn't settle till she got to the bottom of it.

***

Tuesday 18th June 1996 – Evening

John's recent phone conversation with Rita was still on his mind when he arrived at work that evening.

"We'll have to stop meeting like this," said Janet, catching his attention as he stepped into the lift.

"Oh, hi Janet. Alright?" John responded.

"Not too bad," she said, "Although it's a bit hectic on the team at the moment. DI Collins is going mad to find this missing child."

John didn't let on that Daniel was his nephew. He could do without the pitying looks and words of sympathy right now. But he was curious.

"Are you making any headway?" he asked.

"No, we were holding a man, a bloody paedophile, but we had to let him go. Not enough evidence."

"Really?"

"Yeah. The DI's not too pleased, but what can you do?"

"Does the DI think he's your man then?"

"Could be. He was hanging about the hospital when the child disappeared. And the previous day too. And he's a local."

"Sounds suspicious to me." John pretended to mull the facts over in his mind as though he was just an intrigued officer. "So you're saying he lives near the hospital?"

"Oh yeah. On the Riverhill Estate."

The mention of the Riverhill focused John's attention even more.

"The Riverhill?" he asked.

"Yeah. Know it, do you?"

"Oh yeah, we've had plenty of problems with the Riverhill. We raided a house just the other week on Sandicroft Way. He's definitely in bad company, anyway."

Again, John omitted to mention that he was brought up on the estate.

"He's at the other side of the estate," said Janet. "Spinner Avenue."

"Spinner. Yeah, I know Spinner. Near that pub, what's its name?"

"I know the one you mean: the Brown Cow. He's at the far end though, near to Portsmouth Road.

"Aah, right."

They remained silent for several seconds until the lift stopped and Janet got out.

"See you, John," she said.

"See you. And good luck with the case. I hope you find him."

***

Wednesday 19th June 1996

The visit to Irene was troubling Joan. Irene's reaction to the news of Daniel's disappearance was strange. Instead of displaying sadness, she had been more interested in their feelings about Rita taking him to Greece. She raised the matter again with Ged, but skirted around the issue, wary of annoying him if she accused Irene outright. After all, as far as Ged was concerned, the subject was now dropped.

"She's a funny one your Irene, isn't she?" Joan asked.

"What d'you mean?"

"A bit obsessive about that house, isn't she? When you think about it, I'm surprised we even suspected her …"

"*You* suspected her," Ged interrupted.

"Alright. Well, like I was saying, now we've been to see her, I can't imagine her with a child. Not in a house like that. She'd be too frightened of it messing the place up."

"Oh aye, she'd have a bleedin' nervous breakdown." Ged paused for a moment, pensive, then added, "Mind you, she wanted kids."

"You're joking?"

"No, straight up. Have I never told you? She was engaged to be married at one time. She was with him a while too until he pissed off on her."

"Really?" asked Joan. "Maybe that's why she's so obsessed with the house, because there's not much else in her life."

"Maybe. I think her trouble is, she could do with someone giving her a good seeing to."

"Oh Ged, you dirty sod," laughed Joan. Then, bringing the conversation back on track, she added, "I wonder what kind of parent she would have been … whether she would have been really strict. Or maybe she'd have been a different person if she had kids. Maybe she's just like she is 'cos she's bitter."

"I doubt it. She's always been the same. She was a right bitch when we were kids. I think she just saw me as a pain in the arse because I was a lot younger than her. She was always giving me a slap if I said the wrong thing."

Joan could well imagine how irritating he was as a child, but she played along. "Really?" she asked. "That's a bit out of order, isn't it?"

"Oh aye, she even locked me in the loo once because she said I was getting on her nerves. My mam went bleedin' mad when she found me in there."

"Jesus, Ged! She sounds like a right psycho. I hope she *hasn't* got Daniel if that's how she treats kids."

"Relax, will yer? I've told yer, I had a scan round the house. There's no one there but her. Besides, like you say, why would she want a kid in her precious house?"

"I don't know. Maybe she thinks she's doing us a favour. Imagine if she came here with him once Rita was back in Greece."

"Turn it in, Joan. Now you're just being fuckin' ridiculous!" shouted Ged. "I've told you, our Irene hasn't got him. Full stop."

Joan knew she'd pushed things far enough so she left it for now. She was still uneasy though. There was something about the way Ged got on the defensive so quickly. She had a feeling there was something he wasn't telling her. But she had no idea what it was.

Chapter 15

Maurice had arrived home the previous evening, exhausted after hours of extensive police questioning. After a busy day exploring the local area, he was enjoying a few peaceful moments re-familiarising himself with his new home when he heard someone knocking. He sighed and dragged himself from his chair to see who it could be.

Maurice wasn't in the best of moods when he swung the front door open. On spotting a stranger, he prepared himself to stop any attempts at sales patter and get rid of him as quickly as possible. But the man didn't speak. Before Maurice had a chance to react, he charged into his home, pushing him so viciously that he stumbled backwards. Then he shut the door, away from prying eyes.

The blood drained from Maurice's face on realising he had been found. He knew this day would come. They always found out where he lived sooner or later. But this character was particularly menacing. He shoved Maurice up against the wall with one hand round his throat and the other over his mouth. His attacker was big and intimidating with a fervour that suggested things were personal.

"Right, I'm gonna take my hand away from your mouth," he said, "but you scream for help and you've fuckin' had it, OK?"

Maurice nodded.

As soon as the man removed his hand, Maurice began crying, "Don't hurt me, please don't hurt me."

The tears streamed down his face mingling with mucus from his nose. This pitiful sight seemed to inflame the man more as he slammed his fist into Maurice's face then wiped his smeared knuckles on Maurice's clothing in disgust.

"Shut your snivelling, you cowardly bastard!" he shouted. With one hand still around Maurice's throat, he smacked him repeatedly about the head. "I wanna know where Daniel is, so you better start fuckin' talking!"

"I don't know," Maurice cried as the man's hand tightened round his throat.

"You fuckin' liar! The police haven't been holding you for nothing."

Slam! The man was now aiming blows at his stomach. Maurice's reflexes were urging him to crouch, but the man still had his throat in a stranglehold.

He tried to reply although he was winded and the man's hand was constricting his throat. Thankfully, he eased the pressure a little so he could speak. "They didn't arrest me. It was only for questioning," he spluttered.

"And why were they questioning *you*?"

"I don't know," Maurice whimpered. Then, guessing that the man must know something to have found his address, he added, "Maybe it's 'cos of … of… what I've done in the past … but I swear I'm not like that anymore."

The man didn't look convinced, so Maurice continued. "It's always the same with the cops. They pull in anyone with a record if a kid goes missing."

"Anyone with a record for messing with kids, don't you mean?"

He nodded, shamefaced.

"Well I don't fuckin' believe you! Once a paedo, always a paedo as far as I'm concerned."

The man then released his hand from Maurice's throat while he reached into his pocket, bringing out a length of flexible wire.

"Take off your jumper and turn round," he instructed.

Maurice hesitated for a moment, then the man grabbed hold of his arm spinning him so viciously that he complied. Once Maurice had removed his pullover the man secured his hands then trailed the wire down to his feet and secured them. He rolled up the pullover to use as a gag, which he tied in place using the sleeves and an additional piece of flexible wire to secure it into position.

Maurice feared that he would torture him then leave him tied up but instead he began searching the house. He could hear him rushing around and slamming doors upstairs, and when he had covered every room he returned and booted Maurice in the shins several times. Maurice howled into the gag as wave after wave of pain shot through his legs.

"Where have you hidden him?" the man demanded.

Maurice shook his head, unable to speak because of the gag.

"I hope you're not lying to me and you haven't got him at some mate's house," the man said as he grabbed Maurice by the throat again and kept banging his head against the wall. He was so close that Maurice could see the anger and hatred in his eyes, and feel him breathing heavily into his face.

"You ready to fuckin' talk yet?" he asked, raining punches on Maurice's head and torso.

He then untied the gag, and Maurice resumed his desperate protestations. "I swear I haven't got him," he cried.

The man left him for a few moments, disappearing into the kitchen. He returned carrying a pair of scissors. Maurice squirmed as he approached him with the scissors open. "No, please!" he begged, but to his surprise the man cut loose the ties that were binding his hands together.

"You can do the rest," he said, dumping the scissors on the stairwell on his way out before adding a few parting words. "If you're lying to me, I swear I'll be back and I'll finish the fuckin' job off."

The beating had been savage but Maurice drew comfort from the fact that his attacker seemed to have a personal interest in the missing child. This could mean he wasn't a random paedophile hater, and it might therefore have been an isolated attack. However, all hopes of this vanished when Maurice overheard the man speak to a neighbour before he made his getaway.

"Keep your eyes on your kids, love. You've got a paedophile living next door."

Maurice dropped to the floor and wept renewed tears at the realisation of what lay ahead now word was out.

***

Wednesday 19th June 1996
When John came home he couldn't spot Paula straightaway. Hearing movement from the back of the house, he assumed she was in the kitchen and shouted a greeting, "Hi love, it's only me," before racing upstairs to the bathroom.

Once there, he removed his blood-spattered clothing and washed the blood and mucus off his hands. He had already taken off his disguise before reaching home: a false goatee and moustache, and a baseball cap. Although not very original, it should stop him getting recognised if he needed to attend a callout in that area.

Then he went to the bedroom where he changed his pullover and concealed the incriminating garments behind the wardrobe. Hopefully Paula wouldn't find them there. He would decide what to do with them when she was out of the house.

A few minutes later he waltzed into the kitchen, adopted

an air of nonchalance and gave Paula a peck on the cheek.

"That's more like it," she teased. "I was beginning to think you'd gone off me for a minute."

"What d'you mean?"

"Didn't bother coming to see me, no kiss, no cuddle, just straight upstairs," she said, sticking out her bottom lip in mock petulance.

"Ah," he smiled. "Sorry about that. I was desperate for the loo."

"Desperate for a change of clothes too by the looks of it. You didn't have those on when you went out earlier."

"No, I er, I fancied a bit of a freshen up. It's been a hectic day. God Paula, what is this, twenty questions?"

"Just taking an interest in my better half," she smiled.

"Nice to hear it," he laughed, giving her another quick kiss before retiring to the living room.

Once there he heaved a sigh of relief. He preferred it if Paula didn't find out what he was up to today. He actually preferred it if nobody found out what he was up to; neither his wife, his sister nor his best mate. He wasn't proud of it but it was something he felt he needed to do.

The prompting by Tony to do something, together with Rita's pleas for help, had made him feel as though he didn't have a choice. If Daniel had come to harm at that man's hands while he sat back and did nothing, he would never have forgiven himself.

So he'd acted against protocol. Having discovered from Janet where Maurice James lived, it wasn't difficult to find out from Maurice's neighbours whether anyone by that name had moved into the area.

John decided beforehand to use some form of threat to get the paedophile to talk, yet he hadn't intended to go quite so far. But the man was a typical bully: a scrawny, pallid, inadequate wimp. The sight of that bastard snivelling and begging really got to John.

Maurice James was probably the type of man who got off on bullying small children, but when he was on the receiving end, he was a total coward. It brought to mind all those kids who must have cried for mercy at that monster's hands. And would they have received any mercy? Not a chance! That was when John had snapped.

He hadn't meant to tell the neighbour about the paedophile either. He knew that once people knew, Maurice James would be persecuted, and everyone on the estate would make his life a misery. But John was still fired up at that point. He couldn't stand the thought of young children living next door to a paedophile, and their parents not having a clue.

Although he regretted getting so carried away, at least he now felt pretty certain that Maurice James wasn't the man who had Daniel. Well, as certain as he could feel.

Maurice James would have owned up to anything to save his own skin. Unless, of course, he was even more devious than John had given him credit for.

Chapter 16

Wednesday 19th June 1996

It was three days since Daniel had gone missing. Rita and Yansis had discussed his disappearance indefatigably, running through various possible scenarios. These ranged from Daniel returning home relatively unscathed to the unthinkable. And even though some scenarios were torturous, Rita couldn't help but visit them in her mind.

They were both having difficulty sleeping, and were downing large amounts of alcohol in the evenings to numb the pain. Meanwhile, Julie continued to offer endless cups of tea and coffee, and wholesome meals, while expressing concern about their welfare. They both bore the signs of stress, their faces pale and etched with worry lines; the dark circles evident under their eyes.

Rita was also still having flashbacks of her sister's traumatic death, and the frightening sight of Leroy's tormenting face. Anxiety over Daniel was making the flashbacks more frequent. Despite this, she was trying to put them out of her mind and stay positive. She kept telling herself that she couldn't let her outlook be affected by what had happened to Jenny. It was taking all of Rita's tremendous strength of character to pull her through.

Currently, Rita was going through one of her pacing sessions, running her hands frantically through her hair as she voiced her worries to Yansis. Even he was no longer composed and, as they thrashed through the details, they fed each other's anxieties.

"I'll ring that DI again," said Rita. "Maybe he'll be able to tell us something by now."

"It is worth a try," said Yansis. "But perhaps he would have contacted us if there was anything to tell."

"What, like he did yesterday when they had that paedo in for questioning?"

Without waiting for a response, she called up his number, which she had entered into her phone's memory.

"Can I speak to DI Collins please?"

"I'm afraid he's busy at the moment. Can I take a message or get him to call you back?" said the woman on the other end of the phone.

"No, I need to speak to him now. It's important."

"I'm afraid he …"

Rita cut in, "Will you tell him it's Mrs Christos, please? The mother of Daniel Christos. And I need to speak to him."

On hearing her name, the person on the phone became more cooperative, "I'll go and see if I can disturb him."

When Rita heard DI Collins answer the phone, she realised that she had got his hopes up. He must have assumed that she was calling with news for him rather than the opposite.

Rita thought she detected a weary sigh as he responded to her enquiry. "Mrs Christos, I'm sorry but we don't have any news yet. As I've told you previously, we're doing everything we can, and we'll be in touch as soon as we have anything to report."

"What about the paedophile? Are you still holding him?"

"No, we are no longer holding Maurice James."

She noticed how he emphasised the paedophile's name before he continued.

"There was insufficient evidence with which to charge him although I can assure you that we have carried out thorough checks."

"Right, will you let us know as soon as you know

anything then, anything at all?"

"Certainly, and if you think of something that might help, Mrs Christos, please give us a call. No matter how insignificant it may seem, it might just be the final piece of the jigsaw."

"Sure," muttered Rita.

"I just want to reassure you, Mrs Christos, that we are doing all we can to find your son. My officers are working flat out, and there's nothing I'd like more than to return Daniel safely to you."

Rita finished the call. Yet again, she could feel her emotions taking over. Ironically, despite her mistrust of the police, she believed him when he said he wanted to return Daniel safely. But for some reason that made her feel worse. Despite the DI's assurances, Rita wasn't stupid. She knew that the longer a child was missing, the less chance there was of finding him alive. And it was now three days.

***

Wednesday 19th June 1996 - Daniel

The days dragged for Daniel. Fear was his only companion. Since they arrived at the house he had spent all his time in the cellar. Its stark interior with cold, stone floors and earthy brick walls offered little in the way of comfort. He stayed on a battered old mattress for most of the time, clinging to a shabby blanket.

The man had led Daniel into the cellar, dragging him by his arm. His fingers dug talon-like into the wounded flesh, and Daniel screeched with pain. Interpreting his cries as a sign of disobedience, the man shouted and cursed at him, then gripped his injured arm even tighter.

It was enough to silence Daniel who was plunged,

sobbing, into his austere dungeon. Panic assailed him at the plethora of terrors he was forced to confront. Isolation. A fear of spiders. The gloominess of the enclosed room, which cast startling shadows along the coarse walls and floor. And a painful wound, oozing blood through an unsecured dressing.

The man, and sometimes the woman, visited a few times a day to deliver food, and change the pot that stood in a corner of the cellar. But the stench from the pot remained. Heavy and cloying, it hung about the room, adding to Daniel's discomfort.

When the dressing fell off completely, Daniel plucked up the courage to ask for another plaster, his voice trembling. The man looked at him scornfully, and laughed. Without examining the wound, he said, "Don't be such a cry baby!" and walked away from the cellar, chuckling to himself.

***

Friday 21st June 1996 - Afternoon
Maurice read through the newspaper article once more. The media coverage on Daniel's disappearance fascinated him: the endless speculations, professional opinions and background information. He couldn't get enough of it.

He must curb his excitement for a while though as it would soon be time to attend his appointment with his probation officer. Maurice wasn't looking forward to it. It wasn't so much the appointment itself but the trip there. Having to step outside the house. He dreaded having to go anywhere.

Since his attack on Wednesday evening he had been terrorised. He wished his attacker hadn't said anything to his neighbour. Now, not only would the neighbours have nothing to do with him, but he was subjected to malicious and cruel taunts whenever he left the house.

Even inside his home he didn't feel safe. The previous night, once it became dark, he could hear stones and bricks being hurled at the doors and windows. Youths shouted abuse through the letter box. There were also other sounds which he couldn't always identify. He could only guess that they represented some form of wanton vandalism to his property.

Today he hadn't yet ventured outdoors, deciding to wait until leaving for his appointment. He would have preferred to go in the morning when fewer people were up and about, but he'd been given an afternoon appointment. So he didn't have a choice in the matter.

As he left his house, he scanned the street to make sure nobody was around. Unfortunately, one of his neighbours over the road, a young mother of three children, spotted him. He took a cursory glance at his home, which was noted by the neighbour who shouted, "Yes, that's what you are. We don't want the likes of you round here, so bugger off!"

He didn't react. He'd found through previous experience that it was best to ignore the taunts and sneers. If he responded it would only make matters worse. It was difficult to ignore the graffiti scrawled across his house though, and he was horrified when he caught sight of it.

The misspelt words 'beest' and 'peedo' were spray-painted on the wall, with each word covering a width of around two metres. The poor spellings would have been laughable if they hadn't been so threatening.

His first priority now was to get out of the area as quick as he could. Once he had attended his appointment he could think about how he would deal with the graffiti issue. It wasn't a prospect he relished. A mental image flitted through his mind. Him spending several hours trying to remove the graffiti while people lined up to ridicule him and hurl abuse.

Although he tried to put it out of his mind for now, it wasn't easy. It must be dealt with as soon as possible. The longer it stayed on the wall, the more people would find out about him, and the more he would be harassed. But he knew that it would be a mammoth task to remove it. And what then? Would it be replaced by other graffiti when he got rid of it?

He didn't know what to do; he wasn't even convinced the police would do much to help him. These troubled thoughts plagued him all the way to his appointment, and by the time he saw his probation officer, he was in a distressed state.

***

Anne Fielding was a middle-aged woman with years of experience as a probation officer. She had seen a lot, which had hardened her to the job. Still, she carried out her duties efficiently but impassively.

"You've got to get me out of there!" demanded Maurice when he walked through the door.

"Take a seat please, Maurice, and we can talk things through," said Anne, without flinching despite the sight of his bruised and swollen face.

He sat forward in his chair, eager to find a solution to his problems. He wiped his moist hands on his trousers then pulled back the hair that clung to his forehead. His face was covered in a thin sheen of sweat, a result of his haste to get there on time and anxiety about the state of his outside walls.

"Right, do you want to tell me what the problem is?" asked Anne.

Maurice explained what he had been going through,

starting with his attack and then outlining his subsequent troubles.

His probation officer responded with a question, "Did you not report the attack?"

"Yeah, but it was a waste of time. Police aren't interested in the likes of me. They think I deserve all I get; everyone thinks that."

"I don't really think that's the case, Maurice. All reported crimes are taken seriously."

"But what am I going to do now? How will I get rid of the graffiti, and what if they do it again? You'll have to get me rehoused or something. It's hell! They're at me all the time."

"Maurice, we were lucky to find you that accommodation under the circumstances." She then sighed on noticing the woeful expression on his face. "Leave it with me. I can't promise anything. Some ex-offenders haven't been allocated houses at all; they're still in hostels. You're one of the lucky ones."

"I'll take a hostel then, anything."

"It isn't that easy. Look, I'll see what I can do but, like I say, I can't promise anything." She made some notes on a piece of paper then looked up at Maurice. "Right, now then, there are some other matters we need to discuss."

Chapter 17

Friday 21st June 1996

It was another visit from DI Collins and DS Fletcher.

"You'd better sit down," said Rita when Julie led the two police officers into the lounge and then left them all to talk in private.

"I'm sorry, but we don't have any good news," said DI Collins when he arrived, to quash the air of expectation that hung around them.

Rita's shoulders visibly slumped in response to his comment, and she could see the disappointment on Yansis's face.

"We've had a report," he continued, "… in relation to Mr Maurice James. Somebody attacked him at his home on Wednesday, and we wondered if you might have any information about the attack."

Rita and Yansis both gave a swift denial.

"Do you know anybody who might have attacked Mr James?"

"I can think of a lot of people who would want to, but we don't know anything about it," said Rita.

"Are you sure? Only, from the attacker's conversation with Mr James it appears that his attacker had a personal interest in discovering the whereabouts of your son."

Again, Rita and Yansis both said, "No".

"Very well. I'm going to read out a description of his attacker. Perhaps you can tell me if you know of anyone who might fit this description?" DI Collins continued.

Rita didn't take in most of what he was telling her. Her mind was too preoccupied. She was still recovering from the disappointment of finding out that the police had nothing good to report, and the shock revelation of the attack on the paedophile. Therefore, only a few words registered with her: 'tall', 'well-built' and 'goatee'. But she didn't know anything about the attack on Maurice James, nor did she feel she owed him anything, so she responded in the negative.

After several more questions, mainly going over the same ground, the police officers left. Again they promised to get in touch if any new information came to light.

Yansis had just returned from showing them to the front door when Rita's mobile rang. The tinny ring tone made her jump, her nerves were so frayed. To her surprise, it was Raeni.

"I need to see you," she said, without preamble.

Rita was astonished. Although she had left her mobile number with Raeni, she didn't really expect her to ring, not after the reception she received at her home. However, there was a hint at conciliation in her tone, and Rita agreed to call round right away.

When they arrived at Raeni's, Rita could sense that the atmosphere was different from the previous occasion. There was a total turnaround in Raeni's attitude. This time, it seemed to Rita that Raeni was the one who was uncomfortable. She fussed around them, offering drinks and plumping up cushions, as though she was building up to something.

"I might have some information about Daniel," she began, "… but I can't have you running to the police with it."

Rita could feel a shred of hope burgeoning inside her but she tried to contain it. "That's asking a lot," she said. "You know he's asthmatic and needs his inhalers. If you know anything, we need to get help to him as soon as possible."

"Daniel has injuries as well," added Yansis.

"Listen to what I'm telling you," said Raeni, her voice rising in agitation. "If you don't involve the police you might get to Daniel more quickly."

Rita and Yansis looked confused. Rita was about to speak when Raeni continued. "There's a reason I don't want the police involved … it's my son, Jamal." She whispered the last word as though ashamed to acknowledge it.

"I think he's got Daniel, but if you go to the police they'll lock Jamal away for a long time. I don't want to lose another son. I already lost my Leroy, and I'll lose my grandson too when you take him back to Greece. I just want them both home safe."

"W-what makes you think it's him?" asked Rita.

"He was angry, very angry when I told him you were home and nobody bothered telling me. He said you needed teaching a lesson, and Daniel went missing not long after."

"When was this?" asked Rita.

Raeni lowered her voice again as she reluctantly replied, "I haven't seen Jamal since Sunday."

"Do the police know Jamal's missing?"

"What do you think? I told you, I can't afford to get them involved. They been round here again asking questions, but I told them nothing. As far as the police are concerned, Jamal's still at home. I'd go and find him myself but I'm not so well, and I'm in no fit state to be chasing round after youngsters."

Rita focused briefly on Raeni's wheezing before responding. "Hang on a minute! You're telling us that you haven't seen your son since the day Daniel went missing, and yet you've kept it all to yourself. Why are you only just telling us now?"

"I didn't know what to do for the best."

"But we were here on Monday," said Yansis.

"Yes," Rita continued. "You must have had an idea then,

and you didn't bother mentioning it. In fact, you were bloody shirty with us!"

"No, I didn't have any idea until recently. You don't understand. Jamal often stays out overnight, a couple of days sometimes."

Rita flashed her a look of contempt.

"He's twenty-two," said Raeni as though that somehow explained things.

"Have you any idea what we've been going through?" asked Rita, incredulous. "We've been out of our fuckin' minds with worry. We thought a bleedin' paedophile had him, for Christ's sake!"

"I'm sorry, I didn't want any of this. It was only when Jamal had been away for a few days that I started getting suspicious, especially when I thought about what he said on Saturday."

Rita looked at her, and raised her chin while her face adopted a puzzled expression.

"When we found out you had brought him back home. I told you, Jamal wasn't very pleased."

"This isn't his fuckin' home! His home's in Greece, and that's where he should be. And I don't give a shit what Jamal thinks; he's got no rights over him!"

"OK, suit yourselves. I shouldn't have rung you; I thought I was doing the right thing," said Raeni, rising from her chair and preparing to escort them from her house.

Rita soon realised that this might be their only chance of finding Daniel, and she quickly backtracked. "Hang on a minute," she said, putting her hand out in front of her. She took a deep breath before continuing. "OK Raeni, I'm not happy that you've waited five days to tell us, but we're here now. The most important thing is that we get Daniel back … You said you had some information. What else can you tell us?"

"I won't tell you no more until you promise not to go to the police," Raeni continued. "I know things ... who Jamal hangs about with and the area where they go. I can tell you all I know once you make your promise, but if you go back on your word and the police come asking questions, I'll deny everything, and you might never see your son again. Do you understand me?"

"But if Daniel's with your son, why are you so worried about him?" asked Rita.

"I'm ashamed to say it, but Jamal hangs around with some bad people, so you need to be careful."

Rita didn't respond. Instead she exchanged anxious looks with Yansis. Raeni had put them in a dreadful predicament, and there was no point arguing any further about it. She realised now that it wouldn't get them anywhere. She needed to remain level-headed if she and Yansis were to decide on the best option.

They wanted their son; that wasn't in doubt. But to rescue him they would have to defy the law and might also be putting their own lives at risk. Rita didn't know much about Jamal but she had known his brother, Leroy, who was a ruthless gang member. If Jamal also hung around with gangs, then she understood Raeni's concerns.

After a few moments' silence, Rita said, "This isn't something we can answer straightaway. We need to go outside for a bit, sit in the car and talk amongst ourselves. We'll be back in a few minutes."

She had already anticipated what Yansis's reaction would be, and he voiced his concerns as soon as they were inside the car, "Rita, we have to tell the police. She is a crazy woman!"

"We can't do that, Yansis. If we ring the police, the first

thing they'll do is call to see her, and she'll clam up. Then where will we be? Can't you see? She's got us by the short and curlies; we've got no bleedin' choice."

"Oh, so you think we can go and challenge a load of crazy gangsters, and they will just give us our son back."

"Not exactly, no."

"Well, what are you saying Rita?"

"OK, fair enough; it's too dangerous on our own. But I know someone who can help us."

"Who?"

"Our John."

"But he is police. He will have to report it."

"No he won't."

"Why not?"

"Because I'll make bleedin' sure he doesn't."

Rita took her Nokia out of her handbag ready to phone her brother.

Chapter 18

Friday 21st June 1996 - Afternoon

"Now then," said the probation officer, shuffling some papers on her desk. "I understand that you attended a programme during your time in prison, Maurice?"

"Er, yeah, that's right."

"The purpose of that programme was to teach you to manage the types of behaviour patterns that led to your detention in the first place, and to help you integrate back into society. I want to explore your behaviour patterns since your release to see how successfully you are managing things."

Maurice stared blankly at the probation officer. Hadn't she been listening to anything he'd said? He was going through hell, and all she wanted to talk about was 'behaviour patterns'. Wasn't she supposed to help with things like housing and finding a job?

"I haven't done anything, if that's what you're saying!" was his comeback.

"If you could keep to the questions please, Maurice," she said.

"OK," he muttered.

"Now, let's start by discussing your feelings since your release. Have you had any inappropriate feelings towards minors?"

"Not really, no."

"How do you define 'not really', Maurice?"

"No, I haven't. I've told you, I haven't done owt."

"Maurice, the probation service is here to support you. I'm not just trying to discover whether you have done anything. I also want to know whether you have had any inappropriate feelings towards minors. If that is the case then we may be able to offer further treatment to prevent any reoccurrences.

"Bear in mind that our concern is also for the general public. When we integrate you into society, we need to make sure that the public are safe. Now, can you honestly say, you haven't had any inappropriate feelings?"

"Yes, I mean no, I haven't."

"Not even when you were hanging around the hospital corridors watching the children?"

He should have known that Anne Fielding would have been aware that he had been taken in for questioning by the police. That meant she would also know about the circumstances that had placed him under suspicion.

"Oh, that," he said, shamefaced. "I, I was only looking. You can't do me for looking. I swear I didn't take Daniel."

"Where did you learn the name of the child, Maurice?"

"I read it in the papers. It's all over them."

"Nevertheless, you would have to take a certain amount of interest to have remembered the child's name."

"It doesn't mean I took him. I was just curious, that's all."

"What were you doing in the hospital?"

"I told you, I was just looking."

"Why were you looking at the children?"

Maurice didn't reply. He kept his head down, too ashamed to meet Anne's reproachful gaze.

"Do you think that's a healthy way to spend your time in view of your past record?" Anne persevered.

Still no reply.

"I want you to assure me that you'll stay away from minors wherever and whenever possible, and I'll see if I can find you a place on a further programme."

Maurice failed to respond. It wasn't what he had expected from this meeting. He wanted support, but not the kind of support they were offering. He left the meeting feeling cheated and put upon. All they were interested in was Daniel when he needed help with rehousing. How could he convince them he didn't do it? Even the probation officer thought he'd done it, and she was supposed to be there for him.

Looking for an ally, he decided it was about time he visited an old friend. He hadn't seen Sandy since before he went inside although they'd stayed in touch throughout Maurice's incarceration. Sandy was the only one who'd ever understood him, and had always stood by him. Sandy didn't judge him because of his urges. Sandy understood them only too well. And Sandy would always be there for him.

***

Friday 21st June 1996 - Afternoon
Rita came straight to the point when John answered her call. "John, I need a big favour. I think we've found out who's got Daniel but we need your help to get him back."

She quickly explained what Raeni had told them, and asked him not to report it for the reasons Raeni stated. Then she asked if he would help them to rescue Daniel, but John wasn't easy to win round.

"Rita, I'm sorry but you're putting me on the spot here. I can't take the chance, and I really should report this," was his initial response.

"Oh yeah, you mentioned; your job comes first," she said sarcastically.

"Rita, it's not like that."

"Well help us then!"

"No, I'm sorry Reet. I can't take any more chances."

"Why, what chances have you already taken?"

John didn't reply straightaway, which roused her suspicion. In the few seconds of silence that followed, she realised why. "Oh my God! It was you, wasn't it? You beat that paedo up?"

She heard a half-hearted denial down the line.

"Come off it, John. I've known you too long. I can bloody well tell when you're lying to me. It *was* you, wasn't it? You fit the description – tall and well-built." Then she recalled the moustache and wondered fleetingly whether she was mistaken.

However, she was proved right when she heard her brother sigh before responding. "Nobody was supposed to find out. I even disguised myself so if anyone spotted me they wouldn't be able to pick me out. Please don't tell anyone, Rita. I'll lose my job over this."

"Course I won't; I wouldn't do that to you, John. But don't you go reporting what I've just told you either." Then, after a pause, she added, "Jesus, I can't believe you did that! Why?"

"Why d'you think? I had to do something. It was eating away at me. I didn't hurt him too badly. I just wanted to make him talk, to admit if it was him."

"And did he say anything?"

"No. I searched the house too so I'm pretty certain it wasn't him. That means there's a good chance you're right about who's got Daniel."

John's mistake was to admit to Rita how much he cared. She knew she could use this emotional lever to persuade him to take action. "So, you're admitting that you think Leroy's brother has Daniel, and yet you won't do anything to help us? Is that right?"

When her question met with silence, she continued, ratcheting up the emotional blackmail with every word. "You went after the paedo when you weren't even sure if it was him. Yet, now we have a tip off, and you won't do fuck all about it! John, do I have to beg? We've already lost Jenny to the gangs. Do you want us to lose Daniel as well? How will you sleep at night knowing that you could have saved him?"

She knew she shouldn't have used what he had told her in confidence after too many drinks. But she was prepared to do almost anything to get Daniel back safe, and John was the key to helping her achieve that.

"Alright, alright!" he yelled down the phone. "I'll help, but I'm only giving you twenty-four hours. I'll have to call in sick tonight and we'll get started as soon as possible. But you've got to promise me that you won't tell anyone, not even Mam and Dad, or your best mate, Julie. And if we don't find Daniel by the time I'm in work tomorrow then I'll have to report it. I'll tell them I've only just found out from you, and you'll have to back me up on it. Is that OK?"

"Yeah, sure. Yansis already knows though; he's here with me now."

"That's alright; I didn't mean Yansis. He's got a right to know, he's Daniel's dad. I expect he'll be coming with us then?"

"Oh, yeah," said Rita, looking at Yansis's face and anticipating how he would react to the news. "Oh, and John … thanks. I really appreciate it."

Once John was off the line she turned to Yansis. "Right, we're on. Let's go and tell Raeni the news, but not a word about John's involvement, OK?"

Chapter 19

Ged desperately needed to get hold of his sister, Irene. He'd been obsessing about it for the past few days. He was careful not to tell Joan; this was something best kept between him and Irene. Despite trying to ring his sister several times, he wasn't successful so now here he was outside her home, and hoping to have better luck.

He walked up the path that cut through the small, well-kept front garden. When there was no reply, in spite of his hammering on the door, he checked the window at the front of the house. Everything inside was neat and tidy, and there was no sign of anybody within.

To be on the safe side, he checked out the rear too, approaching via a narrow path that skirted around the property. But it was the same in all the rooms. Everything tidied away, and nothing out of place.

Disappointed, he was about to leave the premises when a noise disturbed him. He turned around and stepped back in surprise on seeing a large, coarse-looking woman. She had stains down her baggy sweatshirt and a front tooth missing. Some of her remaining teeth were chipped and discoloured.

"Just what the hell d'you think you're playing at?" she demanded.

"Looking for my sister. Why, what are you up to?"

"I'm Irene's neighbour. I watch the place for her when she's out; make sure there's no dodgy characters knocking about," she said, eying him suspiciously, and emphasising the word 'dodgy'.

Ged noted how she looked at him. He could understand it in a way. Despite the length of time that Irene had lived at the property, he hadn't met her neighbours. That was chiefly because he didn't usually visit often. So he was a total stranger as far as this woman was concerned.

In spite of the woman's aggressive stance, it amused him to think how Irene would feel about having such a coarse and confrontational character living next door. 'Common' she would have called her. Irene may have turned her back on her roots, but her salary as a doctor's receptionist would only get her so far.

"D'you know where she's gone?" he asked.

"Shopping, I think. That's where she usually goes on a Friday afternoon; she finishes early on a Friday. Mind you, I shouldn't be telling you that. I've only got your word for it that you're her brother when all's said and done," she said, looking at him as though the notion was preposterous.

"Well, I am. My name's Ged. Ask our Irene next time you see her if you don't believe me. What time will she be back? Did she say?"

The woman shrugged, and Ged surmised that any information she had was probably gained through keen observation rather than through discussions with his sister.

"Don't suppose there was anyone with her?" Ged persisted.

"What is this, the bloody Spanish Inquisition, or what?" asked the woman, folding her arms beneath her formidable bust and pursing her lips. "I tell you what, love; if you're her brother, then why don't you give her a ring when you get home? Then you can ask her all about her comings and goings without having to mither me."

She then waited for him to leave the garden. He came away cursing his bad luck. Ged needed to get in touch with Irene, the sooner the better. He'd just have to keep trying until he managed to speak to her.

***

Friday 21st June 1996 – Late Afternoon

"OK, we've had a think," Rita said to Raeni once they were indoors. "We'll do it, but we want as much information as possible. We need something to start with."

"Right, well I'll tell you what I know ... He stays on the Buckthorn Estate in Moss Side with someone called Kyle Palmer."

Rita waited for her to continue until it became apparent that Raeni had nothing more to add. "Is that it?" she asked.

"That's all Devan would tell me, and it took all my time to get that much. Jamal tells me nothing, and you won't find out any more by going to Devan. I don't want him to know I told you or he won't tell me nothing in future."

Rita hesitated before responding, and it was Yansis who spoke first. "That's a very dangerous place. We would be taking a big risk."

Before Raeni could say anything, Rita cut in, "Look, Yansis, we already know it'll be risky. We knew that before we agreed to it. You don't think they've got him in a bleedin' mansion in Cheshire, do you?"

"From what Devan says, Kyle Palmer is well-known on the estate," said Raeni. "I don't know the name myself but it's been some years since I lived there."

Yansis looked embarrassed about his disparaging view of the Buckthorn estate on hearing this reminder that it was Raeni's former neighbourhood.

"Yes, I know all about the Buckthorn estate," said Raeni. "You should think yourself lucky you never had to live there."

Rita got straight down to business before Yansis changed his mind. "Raeni, is there anything else you can tell us? What about his room; is there anything in there that might tell us something?"

"Not really, no."

"Well, do you mind if we have a look? There might be something that will help us. The more we know, the more chance we have of bringing Daniel back. It could help us find Jamal too."

Raeni sighed, wavering for a moment before she said, "You can look, if you must, but I don't think you'll find anything."

Raeni led them upstairs and pointed out which room was Jamal's. "You've got five minutes, and leave everything as you found it. If Jamal comes home and finds out anything's been moved, he'll go crazy," she instructed, leaving them alone in the room.

Rita could smell a trace of cannabis as she and Yansis entered the bedroom. Other than that, she was surprised at how clean and tidy the bedroom was. Somehow, from everything she had heard about Jamal, she didn't have him pegged as the fastidious type. She surmised that the tidiness must have been down to Raeni who kept a clean home.

It was an average-sized room, the walls painted mid-blue and cream with posters arranged haphazardly. A large one of Bob Marley dominated the main wall and the others she guessed were of bands, but she wasn't familiar with any of the names.

Rita did a quick scan of the room's contents. "Yansis, you search the wardrobe and bed. Don't forget to look under the mattress, and I'll do the chest of drawers and around the TV."

"What are we looking for?"

"Anything. Names. Addresses. Takeaway menus even. Anything that might give us a few more clues about where he hangs out."

She set to work, starting with the chest of drawers. As

soon as she pulled out the first drawer it became obvious that Raeni's tidying up didn't extend to any items stored inside the drawers. Now she understood what Raeni meant about not disturbing anything. It seemed that although Raeni gave the room a dust and hoover, she didn't interfere with Jamal's personal property.

The drawers were mostly filled with clothing but there were other items inside as well: foil, tobacco, cigarette papers and various childhood objects such as matchbox cars and marbles. She went through each drawer while Yansis searched the wardrobe, but neither of them found anything that gave them any clues.

Next she moved onto the unit that housed his TV, music centre and games console. She noted that the equipment was all top of the range. There were various shelves around the unit filled with stacks of games, videos and CDs. She pulled the stacks out quickly but carefully, placing them to one side so she could put them back exactly as she found them.

One by one, she emptied and refilled each recess, feeling around the back of them for any items hidden in the shaded areas. She completed the compartments to the left of the TV and Music Centre. Nothing.

She moved onto the right-hand side. Second compartment. In her haste she pushed against the back of the compartment and felt it give. Noting that it seemed shallower than the other compartments, she continued pushing until the small piece of hardboard at the back gave way. She felt around in the area behind it.

"Shit!" she cursed as her fingers touched the metal of a syringe and she narrowly avoided pricking herself.

"What is it?" Yansis asked, concerned.

"Nothing. I almost pricked myself but it's OK." He began to walk over but Rita stopped him. "It's alright Yansis. Carry on searching the wardrobe and bed. We need to hurry up before she comes back and chucks us out."

She didn't want Yansis to see what she had discovered. Apart from the syringe, there was another item concealed behind the hardboard. Rita recognised what it was when she traced its outline with her fingers. While Yansis had his back to her she withdrew the item and stashed it in her handbag. She'd keep it to herself for now. Yansis wouldn't be happy about her taking it, but she thought it might come in useful.

When Rita finished checking almost all the compartments, Raeni returned. "You found anything?" she asked, making Rita jump.

"No," Rita and Yansis replied in unison.

"I told you there wouldn't be anything to help you. I think you should go now. I don't want one of the kids to come home and find out you been in Jamal's room."

They returned downstairs. "I'll let you know if we find anything," said Rita, "But in the meantime, try not to ring me unless you've got any news. The coppers are always calling round and it would take some explaining if they knew you were on the phone."

Rita left with Yansis, dreading what they might have to do, but spurred on by the need to be reunited with their precious son.

***

Friday 21st June 1996 – Evening
Despite the circumstances, Rita couldn't help but giggle when she caught sight of John wearing his disguise.

"Bloody hell, John. I bet that paedo shit himself before you even lifted a finger. That disguise is enough to scare anyone. What are you trying to do, frighten the gangsters off?"

"Ha ha, funny," he said as he stepped inside the rear of the car. "I might look a bit of a dick but I can't risk anyone recognising me. We sometimes have to attend incidents in that area."

Rita smiled before saying, "John, there's just one thing I need to ask you before we go."

"Yeah?"

"Well … If the paedo was picked up through the hospital CCTV, then how come Jamal wasn't spotted? Surely, if he did have Daniel, like Raeni seems to think, then the CCTV would have shown him taking Daniel from the hospital."

"He was probably wearing a hoody. It's a well-known trick. When they pass a camera, they just keep their heads low so it doesn't capture an image of their face. The hospital CCTV probably showed quite a few men taking children out of the hospital because there would be plenty of parents visiting with their families.

"Unless someone picked him out as a known criminal, then we wouldn't have much to go on. He might also have kept Daniel on his blind side away from the camera, so it didn't show Daniel's face either. He could have been hidden behind Jamal."

"Ah, right … the crafty bastard!"

"Yeah, they know all the tricks. Anyway, we'd best get cracking; we've only got twenty-four hours. What have we got to go on?"

"Not a lot. All we know is the name of the guy he hangs about with on the Buckthorn. He's called Kyle Palmer."

"I know the name. Big-time drug dealer and gangster. We've arrested him in the past."

"Do you know where he lives, then?"

John laughed, "No, Rita. I don't have the addresses of all

the gangsters in Manchester, and some of them move around. Often they'll stay on the same estate but they'll move to different properties if things get too hot. They sometimes move into a council house that's in someone else's name, maybe a girlfriend or someone else that they've paid off. They do the same thing with private rented houses too."

"Jesus, it looks like we've got our work cut out, then. Raeni did say he was well known around the area though."

"Oh, he will be, but whether anyone will tell you where to find him is another matter." He directed his next comment to Yansis. "Let's get going. Do you know the way?"

"We've been once before but it was a long time ago," Yansis replied.

"OK, just set off towards Moss Side, and I'll direct you as we go along."

Yansis turned the key in the ignition and, as the car set off, Rita took in huge gulps of air to try to steady her racing heart.

Chapter 20

Friday 21st June 1996 – Late Evening

The Buckthorn Estate was a scary place in the evening. As Rita recalled their previous experience of visiting the estate, she was filled with apprehension. That was five years ago, but the area hadn't improved.

They passed the Buckthorn Inn and Rita shuddered as she eyed the faded wooden signage, the flat roof surrounded by an impenetrable barrier of barbed wire, and the car park strewn with broken glass and empty bottles and cans. She remembered how she and Yansis had narrowly escaped being attacked in that same car park by a gang of youths armed with weapons fashioned from lengths of wood.

"I think we'll give that place a miss," she said. "If we start asking questions in there, we might get more than we bargained for."

"I know all about the Buckthorn and who hangs out there," said John. "It might be worth a try though. We're bound to turn up something in a place like that where all the gangsters hang out."

"It's a very dangerous place though," said Yansis. "I think it is best if we try to find Jamal and his friend somewhere else."

"And where do you suggest, seeing as how we haven't got much else to go on?"

John was becoming testy and Rita guessed that even he, with his years of armed forces and police experience, was feeling nervous. Neither she nor Yansis replied.

They continued driving for a few more minutes, passing a couple of street girls dressed for business. The girls were chatting amongst themselves until they caught sight of a slow-moving car, which focused their attention on the prospect of a potential customer. They soon lost interest when they noticed two men and a woman inside.

There weren't many other people about this late in the evening apart from a few groups of youths, and two men who appeared to be conducting a deal. Rita guessed what kind of deal it was when she saw one of the men give the other a friendly pat on the shoulder before walking away with a bounce in his stride.

They cruised around for a while, passing through streets of run-down houses, and an occasional row of shops. The locked-down shutters protected most of the shops from burglars, but not from the vandals who used the shutters as a canvas for their graffiti artwork. Rita noticed that one shop in particular was busy. It was a kebab shop, which had two cars parked outside, and several customers inside.

Yansis continued to follow John's instructions as he directed him around the dimly lit streets of Moss Side. Eventually it became obvious to Rita that they were going round in circles. She noticed they had passed the kebab shop twice.

"What exactly is the plan, John?" she asked.

"Right, one more time along this road," he said, "And then I want you to pull up near to the kebab shop, Yansis. Not too near though. We want to be able to observe, but we don't want them to see us."

When Yansis parked the car, Rita asked, "OK, what are we looking for, and who are 'them'?"

"We're watching the kebab shop," said John. "It just seems a bit funny that so many BMWs and Audis are stopping off there. And I'm talking brand-new, top-of-the-range vehicles."

Both Rita and Yansis stared blankly at him until he added. "They're the type of cars that drug pushers like; high performance vehicles that give them a quick getaway if they're being pursued."

Rita thought back to the cars that used to be parked outside her sister's house, and it made sense. "You mean the shop's just a front?" she asked.

"Could be. Let's watch it for a while and see what happens."

They didn't stay too long as they didn't want to rouse suspicion; just long enough to confirm John's hunch. "Yes, there's definitely something iffy," he said. "I think it's time for me to go inside and check things out, maybe ask a few questions."

Rita didn't agree. "Give over, John. It'll be too bloody obvious. You've got old bill written all over you."

"What do you suggest then?"

"I'll do it." Despite making the suggestion, she could feel her adrenalin surge as terror gripped her. But that wouldn't stop her. "I can pretend I'm his girlfriend, looking for him. It'll be more convincing."

"No!" said Yansis.

"You know I'm gonna do it, anyway. It's the best way … We want our son back, don't we?"

"I'm not happy about it either," sighed John. "But she does have a point. If we pull up outside, we can watch through the car window. If there are any problems, I'll be in the shop in seconds. Let's circle the block once more first. That way, it won't look as obvious. Once we've driven round, we'll park straight outside as though we've just arrived.

"If there are any flash cars outside, we'll give it a miss. I don't want to run into Jamal and his cronies just yet; I'd rather take them by surprise. But if the shop's clear, we'll go for it."

"I'm still not happy," said Yansis.

"Yansis, I probably shouldn't be telling you this, but I am armed," said John. "And I'm an officer of the law. I can have backup here in minutes. As long as Rita stays in the front of the shop, there won't be a problem.

"If there's any threat, I'll be straight inside. I'm going to give you a number that you can ring for backup. I don't really want you to use it because it'll give the game away, and I'll be in the shit. But, if it makes you feel better, you can use it as a last resort.

"And don't forget, it is only a kebab shop. Plenty of people go there to buy food as well."

John's reassurances helped to persuade Yansis, and Rita felt a rush of fear as she primed herself for the task. "Pass me that bottle of water," she said.

Yansis did as she asked and watched her tip some onto a tissue, which she used to smudge her mascara.

"It'll make it more convincing if they think I'm upset," she said. She pulled down the sleeve of her jacket and top so they hung haphazardly, and messed up her hair, giving her a more bedraggled appearance. Then, she tore a hole in her top to add to the effect. "Right, here goes," she said, stepping out of the car.

By the time she arrived inside the shop there was only one other customer, a man in his thirties who seemed acquainted with the proprietors. She was relieved that it wasn't as busy as earlier. When Rita stepped inside, they all stopped talking to scrutinize her appearance. She kept her mind focused on the task, not allowing herself to be intimidated.

Rita approached the counter, making eye contact with the

large mean-looking man who was serving. Behind him, another man was using a large knife to strip slices of meat from a rotary grill. He paused as he watched her, with the knife poised menacingly. "I'm looking for Jamal Samuels," she sniffed.

"What do you want him for?" asked the large man.

"I can't tell you. It's important, I need to see him!"

"Who are you?"

"His girlfriend."

"No, you're not! I've seen him with his girlfriend."

This shock revelation threw Rita at first, but she reacted quickly. Feigning annoyance, she asked, "What do you mean, you've seen him with his girlfriend? I'm his fuckin' girlfriend!"

"That's not what he told me," laughed the man.

"This isn't funny. I'm having his fuckin' kid, and you're telling me he's messing around! Where is he now? Is he with her?"

The man shrugged, "Not got a clue, but I can't wait to tell him you called."

He laughed out loud, and the other two men joined in.

"Do you know where I can find him? Is he at Kyle's?"

"No, I don't. Best go round there and check, hadn't you?"

"I'm not sure where Kyle lives. He's never taken me."

The man laughed again. "I'm not surprised. That's probably where he takes his other girlfriend."

Rita knew she was wasting her time. She wouldn't get Kyle's address from these men.

"Thanks for nowt!" she said, making a pretence of storming out of the shop. She could overhear one of them say, "I didn't know Jamal was into shaggin' older women as well." His words were followed by loud, raucous laughter, and a response she didn't catch.

"Well?" asked John when she got back into the car.

"Waste of time," said Rita, and she explained what had taken place.

"OK, we'll think of something else," he said. "Let's hope they don't see Jamal before we do. We don't want him to know that we're looking for him. We'd best get away from here before they cotton onto us."

They continued driving around the streets, observing the youths that hung around in groups. In the absence of any other ideas, Rita said, "OK John, I think our best bet is to ask one of these gangs of kids if they've heard of this Kyle."

"OK, we'll give that a go. But you two stay in the car this time; you've gotta watch some of 'em. This area's renowned for muggings."

"And what makes you think you'll be better off on your own? Safety in numbers and all that."

"Yansis needs to keep an eye on the car for one thing. And you're a woman. Like it or not, Rita, it means you're not as strong as a man. And we took a big enough risk in the kebab shop as it is."

"You'll still be better off with me than on your own. Yansis can mind the car but I'll come with you."

"No you won't! I know what I'm doing. Why did you ask for my help if you won't listen to what I'm telling you?"

"OK, have it your way but if you have any problems I'll be out of this bleedin' car like lightning. Watch yourself, they might be carrying bloody knives or anything."

"Don't you think they teach us anything in the police?" John asked, and Rita noticed his hand move inside his jacket pocket as he spoke. She realised that he wasn't taking any chances. He was ready to use his weapon if necessary.

From inside the car Rita watched John approach the youths. They were several metres away, and she wound down the window in an attempt to overhear what was taking place.

She could tell by their body language they were ready for conflict. Where they had previously appeared animated, bouncing around, tapping each other and laughing as though sharing a joke, they now became rigid, almost still. They all turned towards John, watching his approach, standing in a horizontal line, primed for action.

Once John reached the youths they crowded round him and listened intently as he spoke. Rita couldn't hear what they were saying, but he seemed to have gained their interest, and they visibly relaxed when he took out his wallet and offered some notes to the main speaker.

When he turned and walked back towards them, Rita's relief was almost palpable. Nevertheless, she carried on watching the youths who resumed their laughter. A renewed feeling of unease washed over her. She couldn't help but feel that John was now the butt of the joke.

"Gilston Street School, they reckon," said John when he got back in the car.

"Do you know it?"

"Yeah, it's about a mile away. It's been derelict for some time."

"How do you know they're telling the truth?" asked Rita.

"I don't, but what choice have we got? We've got nothing else to go on."

Rita didn't even have to think before replying as she was driven by her desire to find Daniel, "OK, let's go."

"Straight ahead," John said to Yansis. "I'll tell you when to turn."

Chapter 21

Friday 21st June 1996 – Night

Raeni hadn't heard anything further from Rita. It was hours since she and her husband left Raeni's home, and she was worried. She'd tried to get hold of Jamal numerous times by ringing his mobile but she was having no luck. It either rang a few times then she heard an answerphone message, or she got the engaged tone. She didn't know much about how these mobile phones worked but her guess was that he was either cutting off the call or switching his phone off. The stupid boy! If only he would answer her calls.

Although she had sent Rita and Yansis to rescue Daniel, she would rather speak to Jamal herself if she could. Raeni was anxious about the problems it would cause when Jamal came face-to-face with Daniel's parents. She only contacted them out of desperation because she couldn't get in touch with Jamal herself. And she hadn't been able to get any help from Devan. It wouldn't stop her from trying to contact Jamal in the meantime though.

She hadn't told them that Jamal had a mobile phone. If he knew they were onto him, she'd have less chance of getting Daniel back. She knew how little he thought of Rita and Yansis. No, it was far better if she could speak to Jamal; maybe she could talk sense into him.

She decided to try again and, if she couldn't get hold of him, she would just have to leave a message on that answerphone thing. Unfortunately, Raeni wasn't used to answerphones, and when the recorded message played she muttered a garbled response beginning before the tone sounded.

"Jamal, this is your mother. Have you got the child? … I need you to come home."

She was unaware that her first sentence hadn't been recorded at all, and her second sentence was picked up partway through.

Raeni knew her message wasn't forceful enough as soon as she cut the call. Damn! She hadn't had time to think, and she doubted whether that message would spur Jamal into action. She rang once more but it was engaged. Rather than keep ringing, she gave up on the idea for now. Those silly recording machines baffled her.

Inactivity was only causing her more anxiety. She needed to do something, so she pulled out the phone book from the shelf where it was resting on her wall unit. There, nestled between the cover and the first page, was the torn off cigarette packet with Rita's number on it.

Raeni knew Rita had told her not to phone unless she had any news. Rita had also said she would get in touch if she had any information. But surely there was no harm in checking. They must have found out something by now.

***

Friday 21ˢᵗ June 1996 – Night
It was night-time when Rita, Yansis and John arrived at the abandoned school building. A quick look through the car window verified John's statement that it had been derelict for some time.

It was an old building, its red bricks weathered and discoloured from decades of pollution. Someone had attempted to board up the lower windows, but the upper ones were mainly broken, the jagged edges of the windowpanes forming fantastical shapes. The concrete ground was cracked; weeds and moss battled for supremacy amongst the crevices, advancing upwards into the walls.

Rita surveyed the building, a feeling of dismay washing over her. "I can't see them using this place as a base. I think you've been had, John."

"You never know. It's best to check it out to be on the safe side. I'll lead the way. Keep quiet while we're inside though. I'd rather take them by surprise than let them know we're coming. You OK with this, Yansis?"

Yansis nodded but Rita suspected he would have preferred to stay in the car. Wouldn't they all? But they might find the answer to where Daniel was within that building. So, even though her senses screamed at her to keep away, she knew she couldn't.

They stepped out of the car.

The school was surrounded by a wire mesh fence about two metres high and supported by battered concrete posts. The mesh had been dragged down in places and there were holes cut through so it wasn't difficult to find a way into the school grounds. They trod carefully, avoiding the rubble and dog faeces while they tiptoed round the building searching for a way in.

Round the back of the school, John found a piece of hardboard which was loose against one of the windows. Rita wondered whether somebody had deliberately worked it loose to get into the building. John prised the board away from the window and it gave easily, revealing an open space where the glass had been removed.

"Follow me," he whispered, climbing over the ledge. Rita was glad she was wearing jeans.

A few more seconds and they were all inside. Rita scanned the room as her eyes adjusted to the gloom. Their makeshift entrance led into a classroom. The place had an eerie feel to it and Rita shuddered.

There were no longer any desks or chairs, but in the half-light she could see cupboards lining one of the walls. The doors of one cupboard were hanging off, its contents spilling out onto the dusty classroom floor. She was surprised the cupboards still contained old books and papers; this seemed to emphasise the state of abandon.

They crept through the classroom and into a long corridor. Here a strong smell of urine assailed them. The ceiling was high with small skylights. This meant that there was more light here than in the classroom, but in the gloom of night it cast strange shadows on the walls, which unnerved Rita.

In the distance she could hear weird noises; a tapping, and a faint gushing sound, perhaps from running water. She also thought she heard the murmur of voices but it was difficult to tell.

The corridor had several doors along either side, which Rita assumed were classrooms, and it opened out at the far end. There were only two doors separating them from the nearest end.

"Stick together," whispered John. "We'll try these two rooms first then turn back and try the others. Yansis, can you take up the rear?"

They set off in single file with John taking the lead, Rita in the middle and Yansis behind. In the ominous silence she could pick out the sound of her own breathing, and feel her heart beating rapidly. Rita's senses were primed to detect any other noise and movement. Her muscles were so taut that when the ringing of her phone broke the silence, she jumped with shock.

As she pulled the phone from her pocket and pressed the call receive button, she heard a piercing screech from behind.

Rita spun around and saw a shabbily dressed man yelling dementedly. His grimy fingers were clasped round Yansis's throat, and Yansis was struggling to breathe. He tried vainly to fight him off.

Rita pushed the mobile into her pocket. She stepped forward, the adrenalin pulsing through her body.

"Get off him!" she yelled, rushing towards the man. Her action caught the man's attention. He released his hands from Yansis's throat and closed in on her, his face centimetres away. As he gripped her arm, she took in his crazed expression. He was snarling like a dog, and Rita recoiled at his rancid breath and rotten teeth.

While Yansis gasped for breath, John turned and advanced. He withdrew his gun and pointed it at the man. "Get off her! Back off. Now!" he ordered.

John's booming voice unsettled the man who sidestepped, crashing into Rita and causing the phone to tumble out of her pocket and crash to the ground. The man paused for a moment, staring at John through wild eyes. He eased the pressure but didn't let go straightaway.

John continued to level the gun.

"You heard! Let her go or I'll shoot. And I fuckin' mean it."

The man carried on staring, a perplexed expression on his face. Then he dropped his hands, and his contorted features relaxed.

"Do you like Piccadilly Radio?" he asked randomly, before stepping back, his actions haphazard as though he wasn't in control of his own movements.

It was a strange question under the circumstances, especially since the local radio station had stopped trading under that name almost a decade ago.

"What the hell is he on about?" asked Rita, moving

behind John. "Come here Yansis. He's a fucking idiot!"

The man was obviously deranged, and she wasn't going to take any chances. To her relief, he began walking away. She cringed, mentally reliving the encounter as she eyed his tatty clothing and manky hair.

Once she was out of his reach, Rita bent and picked up her phone. She eyed the screen to see who the caller was, but the line was dead. She didn't recognise the last number from the list of callers either. Rita switched off the phone and put it back inside her pocket.

When the man had walked a few metres, he turned around and shouted, "You can't beat a bit of Slade. It's CHRISTMAS!!!" His voice grew to deafening proportions, startling Rita.

He carried on walking away from them, saying, "I'm off to see my mates. I've got loads of mates, me."

"Jesus Christ! He's a bleedin' nutcase," said Rita, masking her unease in her customary manner.

"Alcy," said John. "The booze has probably addled his brain. Either that or drugs, or both."

"Alcoholic," Rita confirmed in response to Yansis's confused look at John's use of the word 'alcy'. After a few seconds to recover, she asked John, "What now?"

"We'll follow him. See if he leads us to these 'mates'. I want to find out who they are. But be careful. He might not be as daft as he seems. 'Christmas' might be a coded warning to whoever else is in the building."

Rita's unease turned to dread. If the rest of his mates were as unhinged as him then she didn't fancy meeting them. Nevertheless, they followed the man, ignoring the adjacent classrooms for now.

When they reached the end of the corridor, it led into a hall. There were larger skylights in the roof, which meant that this was the lightest room in the building. This would have been the area where school assemblies were held years previously. It was easy to spot a group of men huddled around the far corner. Rita estimated that there must be at least ten of them, if not more.

Her heart plummeted. She knew that if anyone came from the classrooms they had passed, they would be surrounded. Their best bet would be to move into the centre of the hall making it more difficult for anyone to ambush them. John had pre-empted her thoughts, and she and Yansis followed his lead.

"Keep an eye on the back of the hall," she whispered to Yansis, "So you can warn John if anybody comes at us from behind."

She watched John, noting his hand in his pocket, wrapped around his gun and ready if needed, she assumed. The man was now with his friends. They had a camp of sorts. Sleeping bags, blankets, bottles and other supplies littered the wooden floor as well as waste from food and drink, which was strewn chaotically around the encampment. The men were sitting around a camping stove on wooden boxes and crates, drinking and chatting.

As Rita, John and Yansis approached, the men watched.

"What the fuck do you want?" asked one of them, as they drew nearer. "You're not one of our lot. Fuck off!"

Rita presumed that he was the leader. He was about twenty-five with long straggly hair almost to his shoulders, wearing a tracksuit top and jeans. It was obvious that this place was used as a doss house for the homeless rather than a gangsters' headquarters.

"Come on, John, let's go. He's obviously not here," she said, the disappointment evident in her voice as she prepared to leave.

Chapter 22

Rita had underestimated John's persistence, or perhaps it was the police officer in him that was keen to investigate further. His years of training in the various forces also enabled him to keep a level head when confronted by danger, whereas Rita was driven purely by emotion at the moment.

"Hang on, they might be able to help us," he said to Rita and Yansis before they had a chance to exit the school. Then, addressing the leader of the men, he asked, "Do you know where we might find Jamal Samuels or Kyle Palmer? We were told we would find them here."

"You were told fuckin' wrong then, weren't you? Never heard of 'em, so do us a favour and fuck off back to where you come from!"

Although Rita was disheartened that they were no nearer to finding Daniel, she was relieved to be leaving the derelict building. She hadn't been inside a homeless squat before, and it wasn't an experience she wanted to repeat in a hurry. She kept an eye on the men as she, John and Yansis made their way towards the end of the hall. They were only a few metres from the corridor when the leader stepped forward and called them back.

"Wait! Pete, here, might know something." Once he had gained their attention, he added, "It'll cost you though."

"How much?" asked John, approaching the men.

"Fifty."

"For what?"

"Kyle's address."

"How do I know you're not lying?" asked John.

"Tell him, Pete!" said the leader, urging a younger man to speak.

Pete looked no more than twenty. He was slight, and had a nervous, twitchy manner about him. His face was pale and covered in sores.

"Kyle's my supplier," he said.

John sighed, turning to Rita. "This is costing me a bloody fortune."

"It's alright John, we'll get it," she said.

Remembering that she had left her handbag at home so it wouldn't get in the way, she asked Yansis to find the cash.

"Hang on," said John, then he instructed Yansis out of earshot of the men. "Take the cash out first and put your wallet away. Then walk over with the money and I'll cover you in case they try anything. Stand a couple of metres away till we've got the address then let them have the money."

Yansis moved forward and Rita could see he was nervous. He stopped.

"Right, he's got the cash. Give us the address and you can have it," said John, "but I only want Pete to come forward."

"What are you? Fuckin' old bill or summat?" asked the leader.

"No, just cautious," said John.

To Rita's relief, the exchange went smoothly and they then headed to the classroom through which they had entered the building. They were just about to scramble through the missing window when John stopped them.

"Wait," he said. "Just because Jamal and his gang aren't here now, doesn't mean they haven't been here."

"Wouldn't that lot have told us if they'd been here?" asked Rita.

"Not necessarily. You saw how hostile they were. They're

not interested in helping us. They've got what they wanted; cash for their next few cans of booze or their next fix."

"So what are you saying, John? Should we go and ask them again?"

"No, it won't get us anywhere; they've got nothing to gain now. We need to go back and check the whole place, see if there's anything that might suggest Jamal and his crew have been here or that they've been keeping Daniel here. It's best to be on the safe side."

Rita felt deflated, but she knew John was right. If they missed something vital that might lead them to Daniel, she would never forgive herself.

They set off, checking each classroom. The rooms were all similar to the first one; cold, abandoned and unfurnished apart from the odd cupboard. Many of the cupboards were empty but a few contained old books.

Rita examined a dusty hardback volume out of curiosity. In the dim moonlight filtering in from the skylights and through the open classroom door, she could just about read the words stamped on the inside cover of a copy of Shakespeare's 'As you Like It': Gilston Street School, 1963. The age of the book seemed to heighten the sense of desolation within the school, and she swiftly discarded it.

When they finished searching all the rooms lining the corridor, they walked through the hall to enter another corridor at the far end. Rita dreaded having to pass the men again. She was no longer acting on impulse; she had now had time to think about their situation, and fear had kicked in. Nevertheless, her overwhelming desire to find Daniel dominated everything else, and she did what needed to be done.

It was a daunting experience. During their search Rita could sense a chill down her spine and a feeling that someone was following them. She kept checking behind. Her body was tense and she felt on edge throughout.

Rita was also afraid of what they might find. She was convinced that Jamal and his friends weren't here. Surely they would have heard them otherwise. But what if they were here previously? What if Daniel was tied up in one of these dark, dingy classrooms? Alone and scared. Could she really imagine her son being kept in a place like this?

They scoured every room including the staffroom and toilets. There was evidence that parts of the building had been used since it had lain empty. Occasional used condoms, syringes and empty beer cans littered a number of the rooms. On and on they went until they covered every room in the school. The only signs of life were the various insects scuttling across the floorboards, and the men in the hall. But there was no sign of Daniel or anyone else.

The men ignored them as they passed for a second time. They were of no consequence now. They'd served their purpose, and provided their next fix. Rita, Yansis and John left the building.

"You wanna be careful with your PC Plod act," Rita said to John once they were back in the car. "You nearly gave the game away."

John said nothing. They were all focused on their next stop. 11 Hitchin Street. Kyle Palmer's address, and the place where they hoped to find Jamal.

***

Friday 21st June 1996 - Night
Raeni was becoming increasingly anxious. Rita and Yansis had been out searching for Daniel for several hours now, and there was still no news. The phone call to Rita did nothing to

reassure her. Rather than give her peace of mind, it made her worry more.

It was bad enough that Rita had ended the call, but before she did so, Raeni had overheard a disturbance. There was a lot of yelling and someone shouting, "back off". She could have sworn she heard him threaten to use a gun as well.

She didn't recognise the man's voice. It wasn't Jamal, and he wasn't Greek, so it couldn't have been Rita's husband. What if someone was threatening to shoot Jamal? He could be injured by now, or even worse. What if it was Rita and her husband who had been shot? And she sent them there! She couldn't stand it. She'd have to do something.

After mulling everything over in her mind, she rang Rita's phone again but it went straight to voicemail, causing her more concern. She decided to try Jamal's mobile phone again. To her amazement, he answered.

"What the fuck do you want? Why do you keep hassling me?"

"Don't you take that tone with me, boy! I've been out of my mind with worry. What's been happening? Are they with you now?"

"Who? What you on about?"

"Rita and her husband. They're coming to get the child back."

"I ain't got no fuckin' child," he protested.

"Don't be telling me none of your lies, Jamal. I know you got that child. I seen your attitude when I mentioned his name. And you've not been gone all that time for nothing. Now you listen to me. I could have called the police, but I didn't want you getting in trouble, so I've sent the parents round."

"They ain't no fuckin' parents anyway. And you've got no right sending them. I don't want anyone poking their noses in my business. Now stop fuckin' ringing me! I don't live at home anymore; I live at Kyle's."

Raeni didn't get a chance to say anything further as Jamal cut the call. She stared at the phone for some time, angry, upset and confused. She didn't know what to think, and she wasn't sure now whether he had Daniel or not. But if he didn't have Daniel, what was going on when she rang Rita? And why did Jamal leave home around the time that Daniel went missing?

She couldn't understand why he was so defensive but maybe that was because of the drugs. Perhaps he was angry because Kyle's place was a drugs den – oh, she knew all about those places. She'd suspected for a while that that was where Jamal was spending his time.

Raeni was still tempted to ring the police but she knew she wouldn't. What could she tell them anyway? It was only a hunch, and she didn't even know this Kyle's address. Besides, even if Jamal didn't have Daniel, there was another reason she didn't want to send the police in search of him. If the place where Jamal was staying was a drugs den, as she suspected, then he would be arrested and would face time in prison. And she couldn't do that to her son.

So, having finally decided there was nothing else she could do tonight, Raeni poured herself a small measure of her best Jamaican rum. She'd kept it for years and had it hidden away for special occasions. Well, tonight might not be a special occasion, but it was definitely one of those times when a little drop of rum wouldn't go amiss. When she'd finished her rum, she took herself off to bed, but despite the rum she had a troubled night's sleep.

Chapter 23

"Right, I'm taking no chances. This time I'm going in on my own," said John.

They were sitting in the car a few houses away from 11 Hitchin Street, Kyle Palmer's address.

"No you're bloody not!" said Rita. "How on earth do you think you'll manage on your own?"

"I'm professionally trained, remember. What d'you think I spent all those years doing in the army? Not to mention my police training. No offence, but after what happened at that school, you two could be a bit of a liability."

Rita scowled.

"Trust me, I know what I'm doing. Don't forget, I'll have the element of surprise on my side," he said.

Eventually, she agreed to let John do the job alone, but she took a lot of persuading from both John and Yansis.

John located the house. He didn't want to risk entry from the front; there was no cover. The garden was devoid of shrubbery, just a trampled down patchwork of weeds, and tufts of grass that had perhaps once been a lawn. So he sneaked round the back where he would be out of view. He carried out a quick recce.

There was no easy way to get in at ground level, but an upstairs window was slightly open. It was situated above the back door, which had a canopy. He could reach the window if he stood on top of the canopy. But first, he needed to climb onto the canopy. He looked around for something he could use.

John spotted a battered old set of garden furniture. The

table and chairs had all seen better days, but perhaps they would be good enough for the job. He fetched a chair over to the house, trying to stay as quiet as possible. Yes, it would reach. Just about.

John stepped onto the chair with one foot at first, to test it against his weight. It seemed OK. He scouted round to make sure nobody was watching him. All was quiet.

He clambered on top of the chair. Full of trepidation, he reached towards the canopy. Bearing down, John launched his body upwards, springing off his legs and tugging with his arms simultaneously. The force was too much. He felt the chair give way beneath him before it let out a resounding crash. With the edge of the canopy at chest level, he propelled his body forwards and climbed onto it.

Below he could hear voices. They were over the other side of the house. He crouched down low, hoping that no one would look out of the bedroom windows. After a few moments; silence.

Thankfully, the canopy would have obscured him from view if anybody peered through the downstairs windows. And the back door was far enough away to prevent the chair from being spotted. It would have remained tucked in the shadows under the darkness of night. Fortunately, nobody seemed to have noticed that the garden furniture was a chair short.

When John felt it was safe to do so, he pushed the window open further and climbed inside. It was still dark in the small bedroom but someone had left the door ajar, and he could see light in the distance. He made his way to the bedroom door.

The light was coming from a room at the other end of the landing. He could overhear a couple having a heated discussion. Putting his training to good practice, he checked the other rooms first. He didn't want any surprises. They were clear.

He approached the final bedroom, tiptoeing across the landing. A man stepped into view. But John was ready. He drew his gun.

"Don't move! Just tell me what I need to know, and you won't get hurt," said John.

The man stayed still, apart from a sideways nod. John assumed it was directed at the other person in the room. It was a signal. But he didn't know that.

"How many of you are there?" asked John.

"Just me and my girlfriend."

"Step out and you won't get hurt," called John.

He waited. Several seconds passed. He called again. She still didn't come out.

"It's OK, I won't hurt you."

He glanced to the side, noting the position of the stairwell. If she wouldn't come out, he'd have to go in. He stepped forward, positioning himself between the room door and the stairs. An unwise move, taken under duress.

"Come out!" he repeated.

Finally, the woman appeared.

While he was focusing his attention on the couple, two men shot up the stairs. They'd been expecting company since Raeni had inadvertently tipped them off. Once they received the warning call from the upstairs bedroom, they were quick to respond.

John was surrounded.

***

Friday 21st June 1996 – Just before Midnight - Daniel
Although it was June, the nights were cold, and Daniel's cough was getting worse. Six nights in a dank cellar, with

only a threadbare blanket to cover him, were taking their toll on his asthma. And he didn't have his inhalers.

It was just before midnight and, despite the chill of the cellar, Daniel was burning up. The largest wound on his arm had become infected. He was crying from the constant pain and his distress at the sight of the swollen, festering mass. His cries had now become a repetitive sob, interrupted by frequent coughing and wheezing.

He couldn't sleep. The combination of pain, distress and fear was keeping him awake. Convinced that all sorts of evil beings would come for him once he nodded off, Daniel sat on the mattress with his back to the wall, clutching the blanket for comfort.

When he heard the door opening, Daniel's head jerked back, startled, his eyes wide open and staring. He wasn't used to night visitors.

It was the woman. Daniel's shoulders relaxed, relieved that at least it wasn't the man. She walked over to him and surprised him by laying her hand across his forehead. Just like his mummy did when he was ill.

"Here, take this," she said, holding out some medicine on a spoon.

Daniel did as he was told. The sweet syrupy medicine was the best thing he had tasted since he arrived. It reminded him of home, and he cried fresh tears.

"Right, now drink some of this," instructed the woman.

She held out a glass of liquid. To Daniel it looked tempting, bringing a beautiful amber glow to his sombre surroundings. But as soon as it hit his throat, it burnt, making him shriek.

The woman tutted, and pulled the glass of brandy away. Unused to dealing with children, she foolishly thought it might ease his chest. Instead of easing his cough, though, it made him cough more.

While Daniel was still recovering from the shock of the fiery liquid, the woman disappeared from the cellar. She left Daniel alone once more. Vulnerable and afraid.

Chapter 24

Saturday 22nd June 1996 – Past Midnight

After John left them, Rita waited until he was out of earshot before making a move.

"What are you doing?" asked Yansis as she got out of the car. "I thought we agreed we wouldn't follow him."

"Don't worry, I'll keep to our word. I just want to watch him go in; make sure he's got the right house."

She watched John walk round to the rear of the house, keeping quiet so he wouldn't know she was there. Although she wouldn't follow him, she needed to do something. And perhaps seeing him enter the property was the next best thing. Unable to spot anything else, she returned to the car after a couple of minutes.

They waited. Time seemed to drag, and Rita was becoming concerned. She was fidgety. Not knowing what to do with her hands, she shoved them inside her jacket pockets, and nervously fiddled with the contents.

"He's been gone for ages," she said. "I wonder what the bloody hell he's doing in there!"

"Rita, I've told you, John knows what he's doing. Just be patient. He will be back soon."

"No, sod it! I've waited long enough. I'm going in. Are you coming?"

"No, wait."

"No! I can't wait any longer. Anything could be happening. He could be in trouble while we're sat out here doing piss all about it."

Rita had already opened the car door and stepped onto the kerb.

"Wait, I will come with you," said Yansis. "If you will not listen to me then I cannot let you do this on your own. But calm down first, Rita. We need to be careful."

Panic seized her at the prospect of what they were about to do, and she stepped back into the car. "Yeah, you're right … we need to think about this."

She quietly pulled the door shut. "OK, we know John went in around the back, so I think we should go in the front way. If they've found John, they won't be expecting someone else to come in through a different entrance."

"And how do we get inside?"

"Have you got any credit cards on you?"

"Yes, why?"

"Let me borrow one and I'll show you."

Yansis paused, a look of disapproval on his face.

"OK, you can either lend me the card and we'll do it the quiet way, or else I'll have to smash a window."

He sighed and withdrew a card from his wallet, then handed it over to Rita. She took the card and pushed it inside her voluminous jacket pocket before they set off. "Right, come on. Let's go."

Checking there was no one watching, they entered the garden and approached the front door. Rita slipped the card into the tiny gap between door and jamb, and slid it up and down until she located the lock. Then she withdrew the card and reinserted it against the lock, hoping it was the type that would give under the pressure. It took a few attempts before she succeeded.

She turned to look at Yansis, and thrust the card back into her pocket. Then she pushed the door open and they both stepped inside. It was quiet. They sidled up to the front room where the door was wide open. Rita peered inside. There didn't seem to be anyone around. She soon realised where everyone was when she heard voices from upstairs.

"Who the fuck are you?" a man shouted to someone upstairs. She guessed they had found John.

Instinct took over. Rita raced upstairs. She quickly took in the scene. Two men at the top of the stairs, their backs to her. Guns aimed at John. Behind John, another man. And a woman. John, surrounded. His gun drawn but unused.

Without pausing, Rita withdrew the gun she had concealed in her jacket pocket. She pointed it into the back of the man nearest to her. "Don't fuckin' move!" she ordered. "Or you're a gonner."

She noticed the look of surprise on her brother's face before she continued. "Right, now drop your guns."

The men hesitated.

"I said drop your fuckin' guns!" she shouted, jabbing the gun hard into the man's back.

They both responded to the threat, placing their guns on the ground.

"Right, now step aside. I want you in that room with them two." Without addressing John by name, she looked at him, and added, "And you step back, out of the way."

The men did as they were instructed and, once they were clear of the landing, John told Yansis to grab the men's guns while he and Rita covered him.

"Come on, let's get out of here," said John. "You two go first."

Moving to the top of the stairs, he descended them backwards so he could keep the enemy in his sights. Once they were outside, they ran to the car.

"Quick, Yansis, but stay within the limits!" said John. "We don't want to attract any police attention, but we need to get away from here as soon as possible … Shit! That was a close call."

"I knew we should have gone in with you!" said Rita.

"They took me by surprise, but thanks Reet. You really got me out of the shit there. When did you learn to handle a gun, anyway?"

"I didn't, but I wasn't gonna bloody tell them that, was I?"

"Where did you get it?" asked Yansis.

"Courtesy of Jamal. I'm surprised he didn't recognise it. That's if he was one of the men in the house."

"What do you mean?"

"I lifted it from Raeni's house when we searched his bedroom. I had a feeling it might come in handy."

"I'm surprised I didn't see it on you," said John.

"That's because I waited till you were out of the car before I took it from under the seat. That's why I sat in the back, so Yansis wouldn't know either. I tell you what, these bloody big pockets come in handy. Yansis didn't have a clue what I was hiding in them."

Despite Rita's bravado, the shock of what she had just done was beginning to register. "Jesus, my bleedin' hands are trembling. I'm shaking like a leaf!"

"I'm not surprised," said John. "After what you've just done."

When they were safely out of the area, they parked the car to discuss their situation.

"What next, John?" asked Rita.

"I don't know. We can't go back there again. They'll be ready for us. We still don't know whether Jamal's got Daniel; I didn't get a chance to search the house. I think we've come to the end of the road. I'm sorry Reet, but I'll have to report it. Let me sleep on it tonight, but I'm on the night shift tomorrow so I'll go and see Smithson when I get in."

Rita didn't argue. She couldn't think of anything else to say.

Chapter 25

The day after they broke into the house where Jamal was staying, Rita was in a quandary. She had hoped to bring Daniel back home with them, but hadn't succeeded. She wished they could have searched the entire property, and cursed their bad luck at how things had turned out.

Unfortunately, Jamal now knew they were onto him. So, even if Daniel had been at the house, chances were that Jamal would get him out of there before the police got involved.

Rita therefore felt she couldn't wait around to find out what the outcome would be once John reported Raeni's suspicions at work that evening. There must be something else she could do. And there was still a chance Jamal didn't have Daniel. Maybe it was the paedophile all along. Perhaps John was wrong about him. Just because he hadn't admitted anything to John, didn't mean he was innocent.

"I'm going to ring our John," she said to Yansis, who was sitting beside her in Julie's living room. "I'll see if he'll give me the address of that paedophile."

"Why would you do that?"

"Because we don't know whether it's Jamal. We've just been assuming that based on what Raeni's told us. It might be the paedophile."

"Oh, and you think you can go running round there ... It's ridiculous, Rita. He didn't tell John anything, and he won't tell you either."

"He might, if I take a different approach. Beating him up hasn't got us anywhere so maybe if we appeal to his conscience, let him see what we're going through. Maybe that'll make the difference."

"No, I don't think …"

But she was already making the call.

John thought the same as Yansis, and he refused to give her the address. "Those types of people don't have a conscience, Rita. How do you think they do the things they do?"

"Well at least let me try. Come on, John. Where does he live? I know he's local because you said so. That means he must live somewhere near the hospital."

"No, it won't do any good. Daniel isn't there anyway. I searched the place from top to bottom."

"But what if he's got him somewhere else?"

"He wouldn't tell you. And you running round there won't help matters."

"Oh, so you can do your Rambo impersonation, but I can't do piss all? Is that it? He's my fuckin' son, for Christ's sake!" she shouted down the phone before Yansis snatched it from her and terminated the call.

"Bastards!" she yelled then stomped outside to have a cigarette.

Fortunately, Julie's children were staying with their grandparents, but the sound of Rita's shouting brought Julie out of the kitchen. She followed Rita into the garden to see what the problem was.

Julie found Rita taking furious drags of her cigarette. Her body language summed up how she was feeling; jittery, her right hand gripping the cigarette, her left clasped tightly to her hip, and her face stern.

"You alright Reet?" asked Julie, placing her hand on the small of Rita's back.

Rita exhaled slowly before replying. "I'm sorry, Jules. I didn't mean to shout and carry on with myself. I suppose I'd best apologise to Yansis too. It's just that this whole bleedin' thing is really getting to me. I wish I knew where Daniel was. I feel so fuckin' useless."

"Don't worry, I understand. It's only to be expected. Stop beating yourself up. The police might still discover something. They could still bring Daniel back, safe and sound."

"Aye, and pigs might bleedin' fly!"

For several seconds neither of them spoke, and Julie gazed around awkwardly while Rita puffed on her cigarette. Then Rita said, "It's alright Julie, you go back to what you were doing. I'll be OK. I'll just finish this cig."

Rita was reluctant to discuss things any further with Julie who was unaware of everything that had been happening. She was worried that she might let something slip about the visit to Moss Side when Julie had believed they were round at John's house. Worse still, she might let it slip about John attacking the paedophile. Rita wished she hadn't got so worked up, and hoped that Julie hadn't overheard anything she and Yansis had discussed.

"OK, as long as you're alright," said Julie.

"Yeah, sure."

Once she was left alone again, Rita couldn't settle. She had to do something. But what? She wished she could find this damn paedophile herself. She finished her cigarette and went inside to say sorry to Yansis.

A short while later she rang her mother, half suspecting she might give something away during their conversation. Willing her to give something away, although she didn't know how she'd cope if she did. She couldn't bear the thought that someone in the family had taken Daniel, but maybe it was better than some of the alternative scenarios that were running through her mind.

"I was just going to ring you," said Joan. "You'll never guess what … we've got one of those bleedin' paedophiles living near us. It's all over the estate. I wonder if it's the same one."

Rita was shocked. The estate could certainly be classed as local in terms of its distance from the hospital. As her mind tried to process this new information, her mother continued talking, "Yeah, according to Big Bertha someone gave him a right good hiding. The neighbour saw him coming out with blood on his clothes, and it was him that told her."

"Hang on Mam. Who told who what?"

"The bloke that attacked him. He told the neighbour that she had a paedo living next door, and now it's going all round the estate."

When Rita heard about the paedophile being attacked, she knew it was the same man.

"Rita, are you still there?"

"Yeah, yeah, it's just a shock, that's all. Where does he live anyway?"

"I'm not sure. Somewhere near the main road, I think."

"Well, that's a big help, Mam. Whereabouts?"

"I don't know, do I?"

"What about Big Bertha; will she know where he lives?"

"I don't know. What do you want to know that for anyway?"

"So I can check him out, of course."

"Don't be so bleedin' daft, Rita. You don't go messing about with them sort of people. The police have probably questioned him anyway."

Realising that she wouldn't get any more information out of her mother, Rita finished the call as soon as she could and went to tell Yansis the news.

"I don't need John's help now. I've got a good idea where

he lives," she said. "He's on the bleedin' Riverhill!" She then explained what her mother had told her, adding, "I'm going there to see if I can find out his address."

"Rita, you are not to go! It is too risky." Then, dropping his voice so Julie couldn't overhear them from the kitchen, Yansis continued, "It might lead the police back to John. He could get in a lot of trouble for what he did."

"I'm prepared to take the chance. It's more important that we get Daniel home safe. Now, are you coming, or what?"

"No, Rita. I won't do it."

"Right, sod you then. I'll go on my own."

She knew Yansis expected her to back out when he wouldn't go with her, especially as she didn't drive. But she had shocked him. She was determined that she was going. Nothing would stop her and, if he wouldn't take her, she would just have to get the bus.

Chapter 26

"Oh, it's you again," said Ged's older sister, Irene, eying him suspiciously. "I'd have thought it was the bloody bailiffs, the way you've been hammering on the door. And what were you doing snooping around the house yesterday? Her next door told me."

"Sorry, but I was worried about you."

"You, worried about anyone, Ged Steadman? That'll be the day." She pulled the front door aside, enabling him to pass.

"Well, what's your excuse this time?" she asked, once they were indoors.

He braced himself, ready for one of his sister's rants and choosing his words carefully to lighten the mood. "Do I have to have an excuse to visit my big sister? I just care about you, that's all."

"Well, that'll be a first. And I'll have less of the big sister act, if you don't mind. You don't care about anyone but yourself. You've not been round here for years, and now, all of a sudden you can't keep away. That's when you're not pestering on the phone. What is it you want, Ged? Is it money you're after?"

"No, is it 'eck. We're alright for cash, me and the missus."

"Aye, on one of your fiddles again, are you?"

"Aw, don't be like that sis."

"Don't you 'sis' me! I want to know what's going on. Why do you keep ringing? Umpteen calls I've had from you."

"Well, I wouldn't have to keep ringing if you'd answer the phone, would I? It's only 'cos I care."

"Don't try that with me again. I've told you, the only person you care about is Ged Steadman. I don't know how your poor wife's put up with you all these years. I suppose it was your idea to send the child to Greece, wasn't it? Would bringing him up have got in the way of your lifestyle?"

"No! It was what Jenny wanted. I swear, she said so before she died. Joan told me."

They stayed silent for a few moments, Ged shuffling uncomfortably in his chair, but relieved that his sister seemed to have run out of steam. While he allowed her time to calm down, he was thinking up excuses that would enable him to check out her house. Maybe offer to help her with the DIY. Examine the condensation on the windows, and raise concerns about mould and wood rot. Offer to take a look at the cellar too. Yeah; that would do the trick.

He was about to walk over to the living room window when something registered with Irene.

"Hang on a minute," she said. "I know why you're here. It's about the child, isn't it? You think it's me!"

"Nah, don't be daft."

"You do, you think it's me! That's why you've been pestering ever since you and Joan came to visit. How dare you suggest that I'd do a thing like that. Get out! Get out of my house."

"Irene, it's not like that, I swear," Ged pleaded but he was wasting his time. Irene had rumbled him, and she wasn't prepared to tolerate his presence any longer.

"You heard me, get out of my house before I call the police!"

When Ged failed to convince her otherwise, he had no choice but to leave. He could have kicked himself. He'd been hoping to have a good look round.

For the past few days he'd been ringing at odd hours,

trying to find something out. He thought he might catch her off guard, maybe hear Daniel's voice in the background, or something else that might give the game away. The trouble was, after the first couple of calls, she stopped answering the phone. So he'd tried calling round on spec; and look where that had got him.

He wasn't even sure he suspected Irene. He shouldn't suspect her because she was his sister when all was said and done. But his chat with Joan triggered something. Joan was right, Irene was an oddball. He remembered how she was when he was a kid. Perpetually angry. Bitter at being jilted. Maybe she was sad because her chance of motherhood had been snatched away.

He'd played it down with Joan. There was no point upsetting her when there might be nothing to it. And he *had* taken a look round the house while they were there, just like he'd told Joan. But then he'd remembered that Irene had a cellar, and now he wouldn't get a chance to check it out.

He decided not to involve the police; they weren't exactly the best of friends. He'd had a few close calls in the past, and the thought of placing a call to the cops made him shiver. Besides, he didn't *really* suspect Irene, did he? If he sent the coppers round there, she'd go ape shit, and things were already bad enough.

***

Saturday 22nd June 1996 - Daytime
Yansis had pleaded with Rita not to go to Maurice James's house even blocking the door so she couldn't get out. In the end, she pretended to give up on the idea, but then she sneaked out unnoticed. He thought she was taking a relaxing bath.

She suspected that he'd come looking for her once he noticed she was gone so she didn't wait at the nearest bus stop. Instead she walked to the previous one, knowing he was more likely to head in the direction of the Riverhill Estate when he didn't spot her.

By the time he realised her deceit she would be on the way there. She would also stay on the bus for an extra stop just in case Yansis came to the Riverhill to find her.

In her preoccupation with giving Yansis the slip, Rita hadn't given much thought to her actual encounter with the paedophile. By the time she arrived at the Riverhill Estate, the reality kicked in. She walked quickly and with purpose, anxious to find the paedophile and get this meeting over with as quickly as possible.

Rita's first stop was Big Bertha's house. She had been Joan's friend for years and Rita assumed that she still lived at the same address. Despite knocking at the door for several minutes, there was no reply. In her desperation, Rita also tapped on the window, then returned to the door and shouted through the letterbox. There was no response. She stood back from the house, surveying the upstairs windows from the edge of the pavement. There didn't appear to be anybody in.

Next, she tried the local pub, The Brown Cow, on the off chance that Big Bertha might be there. She searched around the pub but there was no sign of Big Bertha. Rita wondered if anybody else there might be able to help. But there was nobody she knew.

It was ten years since she had lived on the Riverhill, and she didn't recognise anybody in The Brown Cow. She toyed with the idea of engaging someone in conversation so she could find out more about the paedophile. But asking a total stranger where the local paedo lived would have seemed strange by anybody's estimation. Not to mention the suspicion it would arouse.

She stepped outside the pub, glancing around her while wondering what to do next. Who did she still know in the area that could tell her something?

Then it occurred to her. Debby.

Although Debby was an old friend, Rita hadn't intended to get in touch with her during this visit to Manchester. Debby's husband, Carl, had been involved in the same episode that had taken the lives of Jenny and Leroy five years ago. It had left Debby a widow at the age of twenty-four, and a single mother to two young children. The incident that robbed her of her husband had also cut off her supply of heroin, which she depended on daily. Carl had been her supplier.

She'd let Rita down badly too, by omitting to warn her that her sister's life was in danger, until it was too late.

If there was any way Rita could have avoided seeing Debby, she would have done so. But she didn't know of anybody else she could ask. And she was desperate to get Daniel back.

When Debby answered the door, Rita was greeted by the same all-pervading stench that she recognised from her previous visit. There was the same atmosphere between them as well; an impenetrable gulf, which they attempted to bridge by stilted, polite chat.

"Oh, it's you. I didn't know you were back," said Debby.

"Yeah, I've been staying at Julie's. How are you?" asked Rita noticing that, despite the stench, Debby at least looked healthier. Her face and figure were more rounded and her cheeks were no longer gaunt and pale. She guessed that Debby must have got herself off the drugs since her supply had dried up.

"Not bad thanks. Are you OK?"

"Yes thanks. What about the kids? Are they alright?"

"Yeah. They're out playing somewhere."

Rita noted that Debby's children would still be under the age of ten and a look of dismay flashed across her face.

"Do you want to come in?" asked Debby.

"No, it's OK. I'm sorry, I can't stop. I just came to ask you something. I need some important information."

Debby frowned and thinned her lips quizzically.

"I believe there's a paedo on the estate who was beaten up," said Rita.

"Oh yeah?"

"Do you know where he lives?"

"Why do you want to know that?"

Rita took a deep breath before speaking, "I think he might have my son."

"Shit, you're joking!"

"I wish I was. I want to go round there and check him out."

"Course. He lives on Spinner Avenue, up the other end, near the main road. Do you want me to come with you?"

"No, it's OK. But Debby, don't say a word to anyone, OK?"

"Yeah, why?"

"It's just important. Please don't let me down."

She felt like adding 'this time' to the end of the sentence, but she resisted.

"No, course I won't."

"Oh, and Debby," added Rita before she departed. "Do me another favour … keep an eye on your kids. You never know who's knocking about, and you can't be too sure."

"Oh, I know. I always ask 'em where they've been but the cheeky little sods are full of lies."

Rita walked away. Debby might be off the drugs but there was nothing more she could do for her. You couldn't change people unless they wanted to change. Aside from that, she had her own problems to deal with.

When Rita reached Spinner Avenue, she sensed the tension mounting. Her heart was racing and her mouth felt dry. She approached cautiously, keeping to the other side of the street so she could watch from a distance before reaching the house. Thankfully, she didn't spot any sign of Yansis on her way there.

As she progressed up the street, she spotted a disturbance. It was at the far end: the end of the street where the paedophile lived. A crowd of kids were making a racket, and a woman was shouting. She drew closer and took in the scene. It became obvious which house the disturbance was coming from. She stopped several metres away so she could watch without the crowd noticing her.

This had to be the paedophile's home, and Rita soon discovered what the commotion was about. It was a pastime for the kids. Chucking bricks at his doors and windows. Throwing litter on his garden. Banging on the letterbox and jeering. The woman was telling them to move on. Rita guessed that she was more bothered about the noise than the paedophile's feelings.

Rita moved closer, and stared in shock. She took in the abusive graffiti, damaged fence, broken glass in the garden and boarded up window. '*Oh my God, John! What have you done?*' she thought, on realising the man was being persecuted as a result of John's actions. She didn't have much time for paedophiles but, nevertheless, it disturbed her.

Rita continued walking. There was a pathway leading out of the other end of the street and onto the main road. That was where she was headed. It was too risky. If she called at the house, she would leave herself open to suspicion for the damage to the property. Apart from that, it suddenly hit her just how much she would be putting John at risk. And she couldn't do it.

***

Saturday 22nd June 1996 – Daytime – Daniel
Daniel didn't see the woman again. He slept eventually, but fitfully. The medicine helped him nod off. As soon as he awoke, his crying returned in response to the omnipresent pain in his arm. His coughing and wheezing were still evident, although not as bad as the previous night.

When the cellar door opened, and Daniel saw the man, he disguised his sobbing with a suppressed whimper. The man didn't like him crying.

Without speaking, the man placed a plate of food on the floor next to Daniel. He then changed the pot and left the cellar, locking the door once more.

Hunger forced Daniel to explore the contents on the plate: a piece of dried-up toast with a thin smattering of spread. Although he had rejected the food at first, he soon learnt that he either had to eat it or go hungry. The aroma of toast mingled with the other smells in the room: mustiness, grime and stale urine.

He forced the food down, helped by sips of water from a grubby cup that the man had also left. Its dryness made him cough more, and he emitted crumbs of half-chewed bread. They stuck to his clothing, and smudged his lips and cheeks. The crumbs remained; there was no caring adult to wipe them away.

After Daniel finished eating, he sank back on the bed, shedding tears of distress as he longed for the time when he would see his mummy and daddy. He took hold of the blanket once more, hugging it close to his body and chewing on the corner. How he wished his parents were with him so he didn't have to feel scared anymore. Then they could take him back to Greece to see his beloved Giagiá and Pappoús.

Chapter 27

John was running late for no particular reason. When he thought about it, maybe he was subconsciously putting off his meeting with Inspector Smithson. He'd been playing out the scenario in his head during his journey to work. He had to be very careful how he worded things. Mustn't give anything away. Nobody must find out about his maverick cop act or the fact that he had known about Raeni's suspicions for the past twenty-four hours.

"Alright John?" said his friend Tony when John arrived at work. "Skin of your teeth today, eh? You'd better get a move on. We've got a busy night ahead of us."

"What d'you mean?"

"Lightnin' raids. We're gonna hit the buggers tonight," said Tony, rubbing his hands together. "Smithson's gonna come and give us our orders soon. He's in a meeting with the CI at the moment."

"Ah, right."

John put his gear on while Tony followed him around, eager to impart details of the forthcoming raids.

"We're targeting the Moss Side gangs. Probably hit 'em at dawn when the buggers are asleep."

The mention of Moss Side drew John's attention. He remained silent as Tony continued his monologue. "Long overdue if you ask me. The whole bloody thing's been getting out of hand. It's about time our citizens felt safe on the streets."

After a while, Tony noticed John's stunned silence. "You alright, mate?"

"Yeah, just in a bit of a rush, that's all."

"Eh up, Smithson's here. Come on. Grab the rest of your gear."

John quickly fastened his trousers and followed Tony to an area where a team of special task force officers were assembled for a meeting led by Inspector Smithson.

"Right. Is everybody here now?" asked Smithson, glaring at John who had just entered the room. "Then let's begin."

The buzz of excited chatter died down, and the assembled officers' eyes shot from John to Inspector Smithson as they awaited the announcement.

The inspector began by explaining how they were acting on intelligence and had pinpointed several properties that gang members were known to frequent. John tried to pay attention, taking in words like 'warrants' and 'teams' but he was preoccupied. He had hoped to have a word with Smithson about Jamal. But the emphasis had now shifted, and the inspector had other matters to attend to.

Smithson organised the teams, allocating specific properties to them. John heard his name called out and moved to stand with the officers assigned to the same address. Tony wasn't among them.

John's concentration drifted again until the words '11 Hitchin Street' focused his mind, and caused a warm rush of blood to surge through his body. His face flushed and he loosened his shirt collar. He recognised the address. That wasn't surprising; he was there the previous evening.

John listened more intently as Smithson called out the names of the officers who were to target 11 Hitchin Street. Tony was on the list but he wasn't. He silently cursed his bad luck. It would have given him the perfect opportunity to check out the rest of the house. He pondered whether he could trust Tony with his secret but then another idea occurred to him.

When Smithson finished reading the list of names, John jumped in before he could continue. "Sir, I notice you haven't paired me with Tony. We're used to working as partners and, if you don't mind me saying so sir, I think we work well together. Also, I'm very familiar with the area around Hitchin Street. It might come in handy if someone decides to do a runner."

"Not much chance of that, we'll have them surrounded," sighed Inspector Smithson. "Very well, you can come over to the Hitchin Street team providing somebody's willing to swap with you."

"Makes no difference to me," said another officer, and John smiled at him in appreciation as he walked over to Tony's team.

He knew now that it was best not to report his suspicions to Smithson. Once he was in the property he could check things out for himself. And he wouldn't have to risk them finding out what he had been up to. '*Thank God I wore a disguise,*' he thought to himself, which brought a subconscious smile as he recalled Rita's teasing.

"Bloody hell, you've bucked up," said Tony. "You know, John, I reckon you get off on the adrenalin buzz as much as I do."

"No, it's not that, Tony. I was just a bit mithered when I came in, that's all. You know what it's like when you're running late."

"Ha, you keep tellin' yourself that. Anyway, I hope your head's back in the game. You'll have to be on the ball when we go in."

"Don't worry, I will be."

John had mixed feelings. On the one hand he was relieved that he didn't have to tell Smithson what he knew but, on the other hand, he wasn't looking forward to this raid. He didn't know what he might find when he got there.

The raid wasn't till dawn so they had a few hours of preparation between now and then. John would try to calm his mind, which wouldn't be easy. He had a long, tense wait ahead of him.

***

Saturday 22nd June 1996 - Evening
It was evening, and Rita was feeling increasingly anxious. Although she'd changed her mind at the last minute about visiting the paedophile, she was regretting it. She wanted answers and didn't have a clue where to look for them.

Since she'd got back from her visit to the Riverhill Estate, Yansis had hardly spoken to her. He was angry that she'd gone against his advice, but she knew that he was also suffering. Yansis was currently taking his mind off things by playing with Julie's children who Vinny had brought back from their grandparents.

Rita wouldn't get involved with the children though. Every time she looked at them, it reminded her of her missing son.

To make matters worse, Thomas kept asking where Daniel was, and when he could play with him again. Emily, who was a little older, seemed to have picked up on the tense atmosphere, and was being difficult with her parents. Rita felt bad about that too.

She was contemplating having another cigarette when Julie walked into the room. Spotting Rita's strained expression and hunched shoulders, she asked, "Are you alright, Rita?"

"So, so."

Rita tried to smile but felt like screaming. Of course she wasn't alright! What did Julie expect?

"I just keep going over everything in my head," she said.

"I know; you're bound to."

"It's driving me mad, thinking what might have happened to him. It's all just going round and round."

She thought about Jamal, the paedophile and Raeni although she took care not to mention them to Julie. However, as soon as Raeni entered her mind, she remembered that she should have rung her. She'd promised to keep her informed, and she'd be wondering what had happened.

"Julie, you'll have to excuse me, I need a cig."

It was a pretext to go outside so she could ring Raeni out of earshot of Julie, Vinny and the children. Raeni answered the phone straightaway.

"Raeni, I'm just ringing to bring you up-to-date. There's nothing to tell really. We didn't find him."

"Oh, OK."

Raeni's response was laconic, forcing Rita to continue the conversation. "It wasn't you that rang last night by any chance, was it? I got a call from an unknown number with a Longsight code."

Raeni sighed, "Yes, I tried to ring you. There was a lot of noise going on, but the call was cut off."

"Oh, I'm sorry about that. We were in a tricky situation. Some nutcase in a doss house was attacking Yansis, and we had to fight him off. The sound of the phone disturbed him. That's why I needed to switch it off afterwards."

"So no Daniel then?"

"No."

"And no Jamal?"

Rita hesitated, wondering whether to tell Raeni they had

found where Jamal was staying. But then she'd have to tell her why they couldn't find Daniel. Because the house was full of gun-toting gangsters. Would she want to know that? Did she need to know that? After deliberating, she answered "no", and Raeni seemed to accept her answer so she didn't go into further detail.

"Look, I'll let you know if we hear anything else. You never know, the police might turn up something."

"You do that," said Raeni. Then she hung up.

The call had been terse and strained. Rita reflected on it as she broke into her second pack of cigarettes that day. It was a difficult call but she could understand Raeni's disappointment. When all was said and done, she was missing a son and a grandchild.

Because of her own situation, Rita found that she empathised with Raeni. She had been through so much, and didn't seem a bad person. The loss of a son was a horrendous hardship. This line of thought brought Rita back to thoughts of Daniel. She mustn't think like that; she must try to stay positive. Daniel was out there somewhere and she would find him.

***

Saturday 22nd June 1996 - Night
Maurice had obtained a second-hand TV set. It looked OK in the shop but, once he brought it home, he noticed how the picture jumped about every so often. It wasn't ideal, but it would have to do. He couldn't afford another one yet.

It had become his evening pastime: watching TV. There wasn't much else he could do. Because of the mob outside his house, the only time he could go outdoors now was early morning.

191

His last afternoon trip out was yesterday when he went to see his probation officer. That hadn't ended well. When he returned home, crowds of youths were already gathered. He had to pass through them while they jostled him and hurled insults. It was a very frightening experience.

So he spent a lot of time watching TV, and reading the papers.

Tonight the mob was worse than ever. And they were getting louder, and older. When the sound reached astounding proportions, he peeped through his front curtains to find out what was happening. He daren't chance one of the downstairs rooms in case they noticed him, so he sneaked upstairs to observe.

There must have been around twenty of them, maybe more. Their ages ranged from about twelve to twenty, he guessed. And they hung about in pockets of five or six youths. Talking, laughing, joking. Then one would break free from his group and launch something at Maurice's house, while the others cheered and shouted words of encouragement.

He noticed some of them carrying cans of spray paint. Then a few of the older lads walked over and spoke to those already gathered. As if leading the way, two of them began to kick and tear at his fence. Another urinated against his front door.

Oh, how he hated them! He detested mob rule. He'd seen enough of that in his lifetime. What he would like was to get his hands on any one of them. Then he'd teach them a lesson. They'd be sorry!

He returned to his TV and increased the volume to drown out the noise. But he couldn't drown it out. It was getting louder. He couldn't concentrate. His senses were alert to the danger. His ears picking out every sound while he sat perspiring, and subconsciously clenching his abdominal muscles.

The stress was really upsetting his stomach tonight, and he got up to go to the bathroom again. Upstairs the noise was even louder, and he risked another peek through a minute gap between the curtains. They were throwing bricks towards the top of his house. He ducked in case they spotted him. What were they doing? Trying to smash his upstairs windows?

Downstairs he felt just as agitated. The TV screen seemed to be reacting to the disturbance, the picture was dancing around haphazardly with increasing frequency. He couldn't understand it. He turned down the volume, listening out for signs of danger. It was then he realised what was happening. The onscreen visual disturbances coincided with the loud bangs coming from outside. The youths were launching bricks at his TV aerial. They must have heard the increase in volume when he switched it up. And now they were trying to take out his TV.

They didn't succeed, and after a while they gave up. He supposed that they had found another way to taunt him, but he switched the volume back up so he couldn't hear them. It was past twelve o'clock when things quietened down sufficiently for him to go to bed.

Sleep eluded him. He was still anxious. Watching for shadows in the dark, and alert to any sounds from downstairs. Every rustle. Every creek. Every tick of the clock. It all spelt danger to him. Eventually, when every sinew in his body was so overstretched that it cried out for rest, he dozed off. But his sleep was fitful.

At five o'clock in the morning he awoke, fearing that he could hear unusual noises inside the house. But this time, it wasn't his imagination. This time, it was the real thing.

Chapter 28

Sunday 23rd June 1996 - Dawn

They were outside 11 Hitchin Street. Hidden in the shadows. Weapons ready, and waiting for the call from the superior officer. They would make a synchronised advance, hitting the property from the front and rear entrances simultaneously.

John had been assigned to the back of the building along with several other officers; his friend Tony was with the majority of the team at the front. Advance surveillance established that there was a stairway at the front of the property. Therefore, those entering from the front would cover the upstairs as well as part of the downstairs.

As he prepared himself for action, John could feel his heart racing. He associated this with the fight or flight response that preceded every operation, and embraced it. He knew that the extra rush of adrenalin would make him alert and perceptive to any hidden dangers inside the building.

This time his method of entry to the property would be vastly different from that of the previous night. There would be no need to keep quiet. Once they received the call, the most important factor would be speed. They needed to get inside as soon as possible before the inhabitants had a chance to dispose of all the drugs.

When the call came, John and several other special task force officers shot off. The leading member of the team used a battering ram to force his way through the back door. Within seconds, the door fractured then gave way, and they were inside.

A hallway ran through the downstairs of the house with a

kitchen off to the left and two other rooms further up the hall. Several of those in front of John stormed into the kitchen while others dashed ahead.

At the same time, officers were breaking through the front door. The bulk of them would swarm the upstairs while the others took the downstairs front room. John glimpsed Tony through the glass pane of the front door, his shock of red hair distinctive through the opaque glass. He didn't see what room he entered; John had already left the hall.

It was a room on his right that took John's interest. He could tell from the door that it was probably a cellar.

The door was made up of vertical wooden slats and, rather than a doorknob, it had a bolt, which could be fastened from the outside. Sure enough, when he slid the bolt, he encountered a flight of stairs leading downwards. Another officer, on hearing him unbolt the door, joined John as he made his way down to the cellar.

There was no light switch, either at the top of the stairs, or when they reached the bottom. As John's eyes adjusted to the darkness, he could make out a large room. A glimmer of light leaked in through a narrow window but it didn't provide more than a vague outline.

His colleague switched on a torch, and shone it around the cellar. He called out, "It's the police, stay where you are." John followed the path of the torch's rays from corner to corner, along stone floors and brick walls. Then, across the room, from side to side, back and forth. There was nobody there. He would have liked to look further; to see if there was any trace of Daniel having been held there. But he didn't get a chance.

They had only been in the cellar for a few seconds when the sound of gunfire rang out. John sprinted up the stairs. He saw the backs of officers leading two men out in handcuffs.

Instinct told him that the shot came from the room at the front of the house. He ran in. There stood Tony. Gun in hand. Still aimed in the direction of a young man no longer on his feet.

When he heard John and the other officer approach, Tony turned around. "I had no choice," he said. "He had a gun. He was about to shoot."

John's eyes switched to the youth on the ground. A bullet hole in his chest. Blood pumping. A scarlet web spreading outwards. Saturating his clothing.

Tony hadn't taken any chances. It looked as though the bullet had gone straight through the heart.

A young woman was on her knees screaming for help, her hands tarnished with her boyfriend's blood. Officers rushed to surround the body. When they pronounced him dead, she let out an excruciating yell, then screamed her boyfriend's name, "Jamal!"

John recognised them as the couple who were in the bedroom the night before. She was too distressed to see through his disguise. He kept quiet. His superior officers must never find out he had visited this property the previous night.

***

Sunday 23rd June 1996 - Dawn

At first Maurice thought he'd heard the sound of breaking glass. But in his sleep-ridden state he couldn't be sure. Whatever it was, it sounded close. Panic seized him. As he came to, he could hear other noises as well. A dense thud. The heavy tread of feet; several pairs of feet. The squeaking of a door. Vague whispers.

At first he remained still, listening attentively, trying to convince himself it was just the wind. But his heart was pounding in his chest, his brow perspiring. Was his imagination working overtime? A consequence of the evening's events? Provoked by a bad dream, perhaps.

But then the stairs began to creak. Those unsteady treads on the stairs. Unmistakeable. And the sound was carrying closer and closer. It was then he knew for sure. They had come for him.

He dived out of bed and grabbed at the chest of drawers, dragging it towards the bedroom door. He managed to pull it into place before they reached the top of the stairs. Then they were at the door. But there were too many of them. It wobbled under the strain as they heaved against the door.

Maurice raced around the room, frantically grabbing at objects to block the bedroom door. Anything with weight. Throwing them. Some on top of the chest of drawers. Some items behind it. No real plan in mind. Just a vain attempt to stop them getting in.

When he ran out of things to use, he wedged himself between the chest of drawers and the end of his bed. The men continued to heave, and Maurice felt the strain. The chest of drawers began to slide, raining items on top of him. His legs buckled and his body folded in two.

When his knees were almost touching his chin, Maurice knew the opening between the door and jamb would be big enough for a man to squeeze through. There was nothing he could do.

One at a time they invaded his bedroom. In his peripheral vision he could see they were wearing masks to hide their identity. Maurice didn't look up. He was too frightened of what they would do to him.

He curled in on himself, hands around knees. Crying, begging for mercy. He felt a thick hand grasp his arm and haul him from the floor.

"No, no. Please, no! I didn't do it."

"Come here, you fuckin' wimp!" ordered the first man. "Come and face your punishment."

"He's not here," cried Maurice. "I already told the other bloke that."

"What the fuck you talkin' about?" asked the man, unaware that Maurice was referring to John's attack, when he had been searching for Daniel. "We're not fuckin' looking for anyone else. We've found what we've come for. You! You fuckin' pervert. Unless there's another paedo hiding around here somewhere."

His words told Maurice that, unlike the last attack, these men weren't looking for the child. They had other things in mind. When the leader removed his mask, Maurice realised that they had disguised themselves so no one recognised them entering or leaving his home. They didn't have to worry about him recognising them. The implications were terrifying, and the leader looked even more menacing without his mask.

"Get him on the bed and tie him up!" the leader ordered.

Maurice shuddered, his face a manifestation of fear. They tied him to the bedposts while he squirmed and wriggled around, trying to break free from his ties. Meanwhile the leader watched, a satisfied smirk on his face.

"That's right, spread his legs," he said. "And his arms."

Maurice was spread-eagled, one limb secured to each bedpost. Exposed and vulnerable. The leader laughed; a deep, throaty chuckle. "He looks like Jesus on the fuckin' cross."

Then, becoming more serious, he added, "It's a pity he's more like the fuckin' devil. And we don't want a fuckin' devil living among us, do we lads? We need to know our kids are safe when they go out to play."

"Gag him," he instructed before withdrawing a large carving knife from inside his coat. "We don't want anyone to hear his screams."

Maurice writhed around on the bed, emitting muffled sounds of distress through the gag.

"You didn't think we were gonna let you off easily, did you?" asked the leader. "Not after what you've been fuckin' doing to little kiddies."

The man paused, his knife-wielding hand hovering over Maurice's body. Prolonging the expectation. Relishing his terror.

"Remind you of anything?" he asked.

He ran his finger along the blunt edge of the knife, then touched the tip of the blade. The knife immediately drew blood, displaying its capabilities. It was sharpened to precision.

"My mam and dad had one of these," he said. "They used it to carve the Sunday roast. I used to love watching the juices spurt out when my dad stuck the knife in ... That's what we're gonna do to you. Carve you up like a fuckin' stuffed chicken. Piece by fuckin' piece."

Then he ran the sharp blade down the entire length of Maurice's leg, to show he meant what he said.

Chapter 29

Sunday 23rd June 1996 – Early Morning

The atmosphere on the way back to the station was sombre. John travelled in a police van with Tony, knowing he'd need his support. Despite Tony's earlier displays of bravado, John knew what he was going through. No one on the force liked a death. It was a last resort, to be avoided if possible.

He looked across at Tony, noting his pained expression and slumped shoulders. His body language couldn't disguise how he was feeling. John sympathised; he'd been through it too. His mind drifted back to the young man in Iraq. The memory faded with time but it was always there.

It would be the same for Tony. Weeks or months, maybe even years of replaying the scene over in his head. Wondering if there was something different he could have done. Some way in which he could have handled it better. Some way to avoid having a death on his conscience.

All attempts at detachment would vanish. He would think of the family, of their pain and sorrow. Of how he had let them down. Because he had shot someone precious to them. And nothing could change that.

When the van reached its destination, the officers got out. They trudged back into the station. None of them wanted to deliver the bad news even though it was a good night in terms of arrests. John slung his arm around Tony's shoulders,

"Come on mate, it wasn't your fault. You did what you had to do. Anyone would have done the same in your position. It was you or him, wasn't it?"

Tony managed a weak smile but John knew that no

matter how many people reassured him, he would still feel the guilt. They trickled into the station ready to face their colleagues inside.

As John and Tony weren't holding any of the people arrested, they bypassed the custody sergeant's desk. They went through to the interior where they would wait to find out if they were required to attend interviews of the suspects that morning. Meanwhile they would prepare their statements about the night's events.

When they got inside, John picked up on the atmosphere within the office. At first he thought it was connected to what had happened during the raid. It was as sombre here as it had been inside the police van. He guessed that the officers were already aware of the shooting. But he soon realised there was another reason for the atmosphere.

"Bad night," said one of his colleagues. It was a statement, not a question.

"Yeah, it's never good when you lose one, but we had no choice," John replied. Tony was sitting at the desk next to him and had remained silent since they arrived.

"I suppose you won't know about that other business if you've been on a shout, will you?" asked his colleague.

"What's that?"

"We found a body on the Riverhill Estate. One of his neighbours called it in when she saw a gang of masked men fleeing the property. From what I've been told, she was more worried about break-ins than what they might have done to that poor sod … Vigilantes, it seems. He was the local paedophile.

"The officers found him in his own bedroom and, by all accounts, they've done a right bloody job on him. Tied to his bed he was, spread-eagled, and slashed to buggery. It was a mess, blood everywhere. Bed was saturated with it. One of the officers that found him, only a young lad, spewed his bloody guts up, it was that bad."

John was stunned. A rush of fear zipped through him. He stared back at the officer, unaware that his jaw had dropped. Unable to speak for several seconds. His colleague returned a confused look, as though he didn't expect such an extreme reaction.

Recovering his composure, John commented, "Bloody hell, sounds bad."

"Too right. Don't get me wrong, I've not got much time for paedophiles, but there's ways and means of dealing with 'em. What they did makes 'em just as bad in my book."

"Let's hope we catch up with them then," said John. "The sooner we get that bunch of vicious bastards off the streets, the better."

He'd kept up the charade, reacting as would be expected. But inside, his stomach was churning. He felt sick. He had to get away. Needed to be alone. Tony knew him too well. Despite his own troubles, he would know there was something wrong. And it would be difficult for John to hide it from him.

As soon as the conversation drew to a close, John made an excuse and left the room. He dashed to the men's toilets, and locked himself in a cubicle. After emptying his bowels, he stood up and took some deep, calming breaths. But his body was still trembling as he grasped his mobile and keyed in the numbers.

***

Sunday 23rd June 1996 – Early Morning
The sound of the phone ringing woke Rita and Yansis, and a feeling of dread gripped them. Rita pushed the bedclothes

aside and searched for her mobile in the half-light. Rubbing sleep from her eyes with one hand, she grabbed the phone with the other and pressed the call receive button.

Relief swept over her on hearing the caller's voice. It wasn't DI Collins with bad news about Daniel; it was John. He'd be giving her an update about the meeting with his boss.

"It's John," she mouthed to Yansis. Then she spoke into the phone, "Jesus, you frightened the bleedin' life out of us! We thought it was about Daniel … How did you go on?"

"Oh, sorry, I didn't think. I just wanted to give you an update before my shift ends."

He sounded out of breath, as though anxious. "You alright, John?" she asked.

"Yeah, well, y'know. It's been a shit night. I didn't get a chance to talk to Smithson. We've been on a raid."

"Oh, right," said Rita, disheartened. She had hoped that perhaps his report to his senior officer would prompt the police to follow the lead. Now it looked as if that wasn't going to happen.

"There's more," said John, and the rest of his words tumbled out in a rush. "We raided the house where Jamal was. He got shot in the raid. Tony did it. He had no choice; Jamal pulled a gun on him."

"Oh my God!" said Rita, trying to take it all in. "You didn't blow your cover, did you? What about Daniel? Did you find him?"

"No, I didn't blow my cover. I told you that daft disguise would come in useful." He then paused before answering Rita's next question. "Daniel wasn't there, Rita. We searched the whole house. I checked the cellar myself. He wasn't there," he repeated.

"Did Jamal say anything before he died?"

"He didn't get a chance. I wasn't in the same room as him. By the time I got there he was already dead, and his girlfriend was hysterical."

"Does she know anything about Daniel?"

"I don't know. I couldn't ask without giving the game away, and she's in custody now so I won't get a chance. But I'm pretty sure Daniel wasn't being kept there."

"How can you be so sure, John?"

"I'm as sure as I can be. He wasn't in the house and, as far as I could see, there was no sign that he'd been there. So there's no point in me asking any further because it won't get us anywhere … Look, Rita, nobody's made the connection yet about Jamal and Daniel. But they'll carry out a formal ID, and once they know who he is, they'll probably be all over the place. They'll be looking for traces in case he did have Daniel there."

Rita knew that part of the reason John wasn't keen to look further into things was because it would put his career in jeopardy. If he told his senior officers about his suspicions regarding Jamal then questions would be asked as to how he came by the information, and when. He would also risk discovery of his unorthodox activities of the previous night. She couldn't blame him though. He had already put his job on the line to help her and Yansis.

"How's Tony taken things?" she asked.

"Not good, but he didn't have a choice. It was him or Jamal. It's one of the worst positions a copper can find himself in, but it's something we all have to be prepared to do in those circumstances. I would have done the same in his shoes, to be honest."

She didn't respond. This was a side of her brother she didn't like to think about, and she was contemplating how to round up the call when John spoke again.

"There's something else I need to tell you."

The feeling of dread returned. Thoughts rushed through her brain. Perhaps he'd heard news of Daniel, and was pre-empting a visit from the DI.

"Maurice James is dead. A gang of masked men broke into his home last night, and gave him a good seeing to."

Rita raised her hand to her mouth, the shock making her breathe in sharply. She then dropped her hand so she could speak. "Jesus, John. What the fuckin' hell have you done, tipping off the neighbours?"

"I know! You don't have to remind me. Don't you think I feel bad enough as it is?"

She knew he was upset, and was reluctant to push things any further. "I'm sorry, I didn't mean to make you feel worse. I know you were only trying to help."

"Christ, Rita! Do you think I would have told his neighbours if I'd have known this was going to happen? I didn't think … I was just consumed with rage. I thought he knew where Daniel was, and my temper got the better of me. I'm so sorry this has happened."

She could hear the distress in his voice, and did her best to reassure him. "Don't take it on yourself. The neighbours might have found out eventually anyway. You can't be held responsible for the people who killed him. They're fuckin' animals!"

"I know. I'll get my head round it in time. It's just been a really shit night one way and another. But promise me you won't tell anyone about what I did. It's to go no further than you and Yansis. My head could be on the fuckin' block for this."

"Course I won't. What d'you take me for?"

For a moment there was an awkward silence between them until Rita spoke again. "Thanks for letting me know, anyway," she said.

It was a standard response to finish the conversation, but she didn't feel thankful. She felt despair. Rita had been almost certain that Daniel was being kept in that house, and now she wasn't sure what to think.

"I'll speak to you soon," she said, then she terminated the call, her hands shaking.

Yansis was by her side, his face concerned as he registered her reaction. She quickly recounted last night's events, then added, "Daniel wasn't there, Yansis. He wasn't in that house. Where the hell can he be?"

He stared at her in shock, and they took a few moments to absorb the news.

"Right, Yansis. We'll have to compose ourselves," she said. "Julie and Vinny will want to know who was ringing at this time on a Sunday morning. We need to come up with a story. Whatever you do, you mustn't let anyone know about our involvement in all this. Otherwise, we'll all be in the shit; you, me and John."

"I understand. Nobody will find out about us going to find Jamal or about what John did to the paedophile."

"Good," she said, giving him a tentative smile. "The police will probably call to tell us about the paedophile because he was a suspect. We'll have to make sure we don't give anything away."

Chapter 30

When John returned home he trudged into the house, his eyes downcast. Paula was already up out of bed, and eager to greet him on his return from work. Her face took on an expression of concern as she read his body language. "Are you alright love?" she asked.

"Not really, it's been a bad night."

"What d'you mean?"

"The worst since …"

He didn't finish his sentence. They both knew what he was referring to: the young man in Iraq. The incident that still troubled him from time to time.

"Oh no!" she said. "Not again."

John corrected her before she jumped to the wrong conclusion. "It wasn't me this time, it was Tony. Tony did it. He's gutted."

He noticed her visibly relax on hearing this news. He couldn't blame her in a way. She knew what he'd been through after Iraq and, at times, it hadn't been easy for her either.

John relayed the night's events for a second time. On this occasion, however, he was careful how much he disclosed. Paula didn't know about the situation with Jamal. So, as far as she was concerned, Tony had killed a gangster, and that was as much as she knew. Neither did she know about his visit to the paedophile although she was aware that he had been a suspect. He could tell her that as it would be common knowledge anyway.

He knew that he should be able to trust her with this

information. Usually, he told her most things. But he was edgy at the moment. Rita and Yansis already knew what he had been up to, and that was two people too many as it was. The fewer that knew, the better.

Besides, how could he trust Paula with any information anymore? She was the one who had told Rita all about him in the first place. If Rita hadn't known about his job then maybe she wouldn't have asked for his help. Then perhaps he wouldn't have got involved with Jamal and the paedophile.

John was done with talking. After such a hard night, he just wanted to have a lie down. But once he was there, troubling thoughts whirled around in his mind. He was dreading the moment when the force discovered the connection with Jamal. Questions were bound to be asked.

He was prepared. When his superior officers asked to speak to him about Jamal, he would feign ignorance about the connection. Hopefully they would treat the family tie as no more than a coincidence. As long as they never found out about his involvement, there was nothing more they could do.

In the meantime, he would have to carry on as normal. He couldn't let Paula know how troubled he really was by the whole episode. She must be led to assume that his reactions were because of his missing nephew, and a death while on duty; nothing more. As if that wasn't enough, anyway.

John tried to reassure himself that he could carry it off. He was used to disguising his feelings; years of practice had taught him how.

***

Sunday 23rd June 1996
It was later that day when DI Collins and DS Fletcher paid

Rita and Yansis a visit. Although they were expecting the police to call in connection with the paedophile, they still wondered if there could be some information about Daniel. They couldn't help it; every time the officers called round, they prepared themselves for news.

Noting the eager expressions on Rita and Yansis's faces, DS Fletcher quelled their anticipation straightaway.

"I'm afraid we don't have any news regarding your son," he said.

Rita lowered her head, crestfallen.

"We're here about a related matter," added the inspector.

"I'll put the kettle on," said Julie, disappearing to the kitchen so they could talk in private.

They went through to the living room.

"If we could sit down," said the DI.

"Oh, of course," Yansis replied, holding his hand out towards a settee.

"After you," said the inspector, and Rita noted that the two detectives positioned themselves so they could examine her and Yansis's reactions to the news they had come to deliver.

Once they were seated, Inspector Collins began, "It's about the man we had in for questioning, a Mr Maurice James."

"Oh, the paedo, you mean," said Rita.

He ignored her derogatory term and continued to speak. "We received a report from one of his neighbours this morning. I'm afraid he's been found dead in his home."

"Yeah, I know."

As soon as she spoke, she knew she had been too hasty. The two detectives sat up straighter in their chairs, leaning slightly forward, indicating that she had caught their keen attention. She had no alternative but to explain how she came by the information.

"My brother told me; he's a police officer."

"Aah. Why didn't you tell us this earlier?" asked DI Collins.

Rita could feel his eyes watching her, noting every movement and facial expression. She tried to retain her composure, but couldn't help waffling. "I didn't think it was relevant. I've been keeping him up to date. Obviously, he's Daniel's uncle so he's been concerned, well worried really. I told him about the paedophile. I didn't see any reason why I shouldn't. So that's why he rang to tell me when he was found dead."

"I see," said DI Collins, nodding to the detective sergeant. "Can you let us have his name please?"

Sergeant Fletcher followed his prompt and removed a notepad and pen from his inside jacket pocket.

"It's John Steadman."

"And, can you tell me his rank and where he is stationed?"

"Manchester, I'm not sure where exactly. He's special task force."

DI Collins seemed more interested at the mention of the special task force. '*Oh no, I've done it again!*' thought Rita. She wasn't even sure whether she should have been aware that John was a special task force officer. Perhaps he wasn't supposed to share that information.

Under normal circumstances she would have been much more cautious, but her mind was in turmoil. From the moment she saw the officers she thought only of Daniel, and prepared herself for bad news. And when the DI had delivered the news about the paedophile, even though she expected it, she had still been distracted. She was also thankful that it was his dead body they were referring to rather than Daniel's. Because of her relief, she reacted without restraint.

"Right," said the inspector. "I think that will be all for now."

The two police officers stood up to leave. Rita couldn't wait to get them out of the house but she tried to act nonchalant.

As they were approaching the living room door, which Yansis was holding open for them, DI Collins turned to face Rita, and spoke. "Just one more thing before we go. Your brother didn't happen to mention any other events last night, did he?"

"No, why?"

This time Rita was prepared. She knew what was coming.

"We arrested a number of people last night in the Moss Side area. Unfortunately, there was a fatality involved in the incident. A Mr Jamal Samuels. I'm informed that he has a connection to your son. In fact, he's your son's uncle. He was Leroy Booth's half-brother."

"Really?" said Rita. She could feel her heart hammering in her chest, but kept telling herself that there was no way DI Collins would know about her involvement. He wouldn't realise that she already knew who Jamal was, or that they'd spent the previous night looking for him.

"Now that's what I call a coincidence," said the inspector.

"Yes, well that's all it is. What are you trying to imply?"

"Nothing at all. I merely passed comment about the fact that it was quite a coincidence."

"Yeah, well we don't need comments like that. Don't you think we're going through enough as it is? If the guy got killed then it doesn't bloody surprise me! If he was anything like his brother then he was probably up to no good anyway. I bet it was just a matter of time. I'm sorry if that offends you, but I've got no time for any of Leroy's family. They're all scum if you ask me.

"Now, you've said what you came here to say so unless you've got any news about my son, why don't you leave us in peace? Go and do your job instead of making stupid comments to decent, law-abiding citizens."

Yansis was now standing by Rita's side and she felt his hand on her arm. "It's OK, Yansis. I've said my piece. Now goodbye, officers."

She was relieved when the officers left Julie's home.

"Rita, I know you are feeling bad; we all are. But why did you have to shout at the police like that?" asked Yansis.

"It's called deflection, Yansis. Didn't you see the way he was looking at me? I don't want them getting too bloody suspicious, do I? If he thinks I'm really offended by his sly comment then hopefully it will stop him digging further."

Chapter 31

"Come in," said Inspector Smithson when John knocked on his office door.

"You wanted to see me sir?"

"Yes, that's right. Take a seat."

He waited until John was sitting comfortably before beginning. "It has come to my attention that you are a distant relative of the fatality from this morning's raid."

Smithson looked directly at John who knew that he was observing his immediate reaction.

"Really?" asked John, sticking his head forward and opening his eyes wide. '*Body language, mustn't forget the body language,*' he reminded himself.

"Yes, a Mr Jamal Samuels. Name mean anything to you?"

John feigned contemplation. "No sir, can't say that it does."

"He was the half-brother of Mr Leroy Booth."

"Leroy Booth?"

"Perhaps you recognise that name."

"It definitely rings a bell, yeah." John scratched his chin and furrowed his brow.

"He fathered your sister's baby? The young boy who is currently missing."

"Oh my God! You mean, Daniel's dad? No wonder the name rang a bell. Sorry sir, I didn't know his surname. I was away in the army at the time, and I never met him. My sister and Leroy both died before the baby was born. Before Daniel was born, that is. Jesus! That means that the guy who died was Daniel's uncle."

"That's correct," said Smithson, picking up some papers from his desk before scanning them. "I have details of the events surrounding your sister's death here. It seems that Leroy was involved with gangs too. They both died from gunshot wounds."

"That's right, sir. Unfortunately my sister was mixed up with a bad crowd; it was a really harrowing time for my family."

"I wondered whether there might be a connection with your nephew's disappearance."

"Dunno, sir. We went through the property searching for drugs. Of course, I wasn't aware that he was related at the time so I wasn't looking for anything else …"

"Very well. Perhaps you'd like to recap on the events of this morning."

John was relieved that he wasn't in the room when Jamal was shot. At least he was clear on that score. He gave his superior officer a quick rundown, providing him with details of where everybody was situated when the shot was fired, and what action they took.

When he had finished, Smithson asked, "So, can I take it that you weren't aware of the family connection before you went on the raid?"

"Of course I wasn't, sir. I'd have declared it otherwise. I'm still trying to get my head round all this; I can't believe it!"

"Fair enough. I'm surprised you didn't mention that you were related to the missing boy though."

"I didn't want you thinking I wasn't fit for duty, sir. And I didn't want anyone persuading me to take compassionate leave. I can still do my job. That's what I was trained for; to deal with all sorts of dire circumstances."

"Yes, I understand you're a very committed officer."

John could see by the look on Smithson's face that he was

satisfied with the explanation he had given. Smithson was about to let him go when John asked, "I was just wondering, sir; because of the connection, won't forensics be running checks on the building?"

"Oh yes, I think we can be sure of that. Detective Inspector Collins and his team were very interested in the family connection, and may wish to speak to you at some point. I don't think there'll be any problem though; I'm happy with the account you've given. I shall have a word with DI Collins in the meantime and reassure him it's just an unfortunate coincidence. I think you and your family have got enough to contend with as it is."

"Thank you, sir."

"No problem, Steadman. Good luck with finding your nephew."

"Thank you, sir. Oh, and sir, I still haven't told everyone that I'm related to Daniel. I prefer it that way. They'd only make a fuss."

"Don't worry, Steadman. I appreciate that you don't want it to interfere with your work."

John walked out of Inspector Smithson's office, inwardly heaving a sigh of relief. Thank God, he had pulled it off. And Smithson didn't once mention the paedophile so he obviously had no idea of his involvement there. Now all they needed to do was find Daniel.

***

Sunday 23rd June 1996 - Evening
The events of the day were still going over in Rita's mind. Now they had got the interview with the detectives out of the way, her focus shifted back to her concern over Daniel. It was always there. The worry. The nagging uncertainty. She

sometimes managed to put it aside temporarily, but it soon resurfaced in her mind.

She couldn't understand any of it. The two people they suspected the most had both died on the same night. She could hardly believe it. But, worst of all, where did that leave them? Where could Daniel be, and would they stand any chance at all of getting him back alive after such a long time?

She continued frantically searching for answers, running over the details with Yansis. "Y'know, believe it or not, I kinda feel sorry for Raeni in a way. It must be terrible losing two sons. That poor woman! I sympathise with her; I know what she's going through."

"Rita, please!" Yansis pleaded. "We don't know that Daniel's gone yet. We have to carry on hoping until we find out properly."

"OK. It's just that it's all so confusing. It's doing my fuckin' head in! Where the hell can he be? Jamal's dead. The paedo's dead. So we know neither of them have got him. Unless … oh my God! What if he was part of a paedophile ring? Some other sick bastard might have Daniel, or there might be more than one of them holding him."

Yansis took hold of Rita. "Calm down, Rita. We cannot think like this."

"OK, OK," she said, trying to convince herself as much as Yansis. Then she took a deep breath to steady herself. "Right, what about my family, Yansis? I know you don't like me to think of them in that way, but I'm just looking at all the alternatives. And, when all's said and done, what other alternatives are left?"

"I don't know, Rita. I don't think they would take Daniel."

"What? Bitter and twisted Aunty Irene? Don't you think she would be capable of it?" she asked, raising an eyebrow.

They soon reached a point where there was nothing else to say. Acceptance of their situation slowly dawned and they clung to each other for several moments trying to draw comfort. Then Rita suddenly withdrew from Yansis's embrace as a thought occurred to her.

"Yansis, I've got an idea," she announced. "I think I know where Daniel might be. Come on, let's get in the car quick. I'll tell you on the way there."

Chapter 32

Sunday 23rd June 1996 - Evening

A young woman answered the door, and Rita and Yansis burst into the house before she had chance to warn her mother. They marched up to the living room but Rita stopped short at the open door. The sight of her son sitting on Raeni's knee, with his back to them, took her breath away.

Raeni looked up from the book she was reading to Daniel, her expression switching from joy to sadness. Daniel noticed the change and followed her line of vision.

"Mummy, Daddy!" he squealed when he saw who was there, and he ran across the room to greet them.

Rita lifted him into her arms, absorbed in the moment, her intended words of anger for Raeni momentarily cast aside.

"Oh sweetheart, how are you? Are you alright, love?"

"Yes Mummy, the lady was nice. She gave me cake and we played games. The man wasn't nice though, but Raeni says he's gone forever now and won't be coming back …"

Rita interrupted his excited chatter. "What about your asthma, love? How is it?"

"A lot better. I don't have to use my mask and nebber … nebber … nebberhaler …"

"Your nebuhaler?"

"Yes, I don't have to use it any more. Raeni says I'm a big boy now, and I can use my inhaler on its own like she does."

Rita was confused, trying to take it all in. She looked towards the other woman for answers, "Raeni?"

"Don't worry, I didn't tell him anything. I'm Raeni to him, just Raeni," she said, her voice catching. "I gave him some Ventolin, it helped with his cough. I've tended to his sores as

well, but I think he'll still need to see a doctor. They're a bit
of a mess, especially the big one on his arm."

Rita passed Daniel to Yansis and stepped forward to
speak to Raeni.

"How long has he been here?"

"Yesterday afternoon," she replied. Then she muttered,
"Jamal brought him here … then he went out again." Her
voice was barely audible as she stumbled over her son's
name.

"But I rang you last night!"

Raeni didn't respond, but she lowered her head in shame.

"So, you mean to tell me," Rita continued, "that when I
rang you, Daniel was already here, and you didn't have the
decency to let me know? That's more than a day, for God's
sake!"

"I'm sorry. I knew you'd take him away as soon as you
came," Raeni replied.

Rita could have carried on reproaching Raeni, but the
sight of the poor woman, defeated in grief, stopped her.
Instead, she said, "But the police … surely they'd have seen
Daniel when they came to tell you …"

Raeni's rapid reply prevented Rita having to say the
words *about Jamal dying*. She guessed that Raeni couldn't
face hearing those words again so soon after receiving the
sad news. "The police didn't see him," Raeni said. "I
recognised that inspector straightaway when I saw the car, so
Corine took Daniel out the back way till they'd gone."

"Why did Jamal take him?" Rita asked. "What could he
possibly hope to gain?"

"He told me he was waiting for you to go back to Greece,
then he was going to bring him to live with me. But when
you went looking for Daniel at that house, he decided to
bring him here straightaway."

"How did he expect to get away with it?" she asked. "My mam lives a few streets away, for God's sake! It doesn't make sense."

Rita heard the emotion in Raeni's voice as she replied, "A lot of the things my Jamal got up to didn't make any sense. It's the drugs that send them that way." She then bowed her head again, and Rita guessed she was trying to conceal her tears.

Rita was still angry, and was having difficulty containing her rage. To think that, since yesterday afternoon, she and Yansis had still been worried about Daniel's whereabouts. She should have laid into her. Shouted at her. Told her what a callous, selfish woman she was.

But she couldn't.

As she looked at the sad, lonely figure, her anger was overridden by pity and her desire to be with Daniel and Yansis. At least she had a good life with them. What did this poor woman have?

Rita turned to walk away with Yansis and Daniel as Raeni called after them, "I just wanted a little time with him, something to remember before you take him away again. Goodbye Daniel, love."

She stood up and followed them out into the hall. There she grasped Daniel and planted a kiss on each of his cheeks, gazing lovingly at him, her eyes moist. "Goodbye my love," she said again.

After a moment's hesitation, Rita left the house with her husband and child. She didn't need to say anything more; Raeni had been punished enough.

***

It was while Rita had been mulling over the possibilities that it had occurred to her. Jamal and Maurice James had always been the two biggest suspects as far as she was concerned. Assuming that the paedophile usually operated alone, once he was out of the picture that left Jamal.

He had known they were onto him when they raided the property where he was staying. So, it seemed logical that if Jamal was holding Daniel, he would then have looked for somewhere else to hide him.

Rita knew how much Raeni had wanted Daniel back. She'd seen it in her eyes during their previous visit. Amidst the sorrow and despair, Rita detected a longing in her.

Given how Raeni felt about Daniel, if Jamal arrived with him, it was unlikely that she would have wanted to give him up straightaway.

Rita was right. Raeni latched onto those last few hours. And the loss of her second son made her even more desperate to keep hold of Daniel. She must have known that her time with him was limited so she'd made the most of it regardless of the consequences. She was a woman torn apart by grief who perhaps thought she had nothing left to lose.

As Rita made the call to the police, she felt a tremendous sense of guilt. Poor Raeni had already been through so much. But the police would want to know where Daniel had been since Jamal's death. And that meant Rita had to tell them.

Raeni would be held to account for harbouring Daniel for the past day. But in view of all she had been through, and for the reward of spending some precious time with her grandson, it was perhaps a small price to pay.

Chapter 33

Thursday 27ᵗʰ June 1996

It was four days since Rita and Yansis had brought Daniel back with them to Julie and Vinny's home. Since then he had been withdrawn; not at all like his usual self.

When they arrived at Julie's, the children rushed to greet Daniel, but they were disappointed with his response. He had remained silent, cowering behind Rita and Yansis, and peeking out at intervals to survey them warily. Rita supposed that the excitement was too much for him after what he had been through.

It was two days before Daniel wanted to play with Thomas and Emily. Initially his only interest was in his parents whom he clung to, following Rita every time she went out of the room.

Although Rita was relieved to have him back, she was concerned about his fragile emotional state. It was understandable though, given that he was away from them for a whole week. The circumstances of his captivity were also troubling.

From the evidence the police uncovered, Rita found out that Daniel had spent the whole of the time in a cellar. He hadn't been allowed out at all, not even to use the toilet.

When Jamal took Daniel to Raeni's, they had destroyed all the evidence including an old duvet that Daniel slept on. It had taken an examination by the forensics team to establish that Daniel spent time in the cellar, and a bunch of hotshot detectives to extract a confession from Jamal's girlfriend.

Apart from the emotional scars, Daniel suffered physically. Rita had recoiled on seeing the septic, swollen wound on his arm, and took him to see a doctor as soon as possible. Poor little thing! She wondered how he had coped with the pain, terror and discomfort.

The doctor prescribed an increased dosage of his inhaler as well as tending to Daniel's wounds, several of which had become infected. He also gave Rita and Yansis advice on dealing with the emotional effects of his incarceration.

Rita was relieved when Daniel began to interact with Thomas and Emily again. Four days on, and he wasn't quite as clingy as he had been. While he was occupied building houses from plastic bricks with Thomas, she rang John.

"Hi, Sis. How's it going?" he greeted.

"Getting there," she replied. "He's a lot better than he was, thank God! The doctor said it will take time, though, so we've just got to be patient. How about you? Everything still alright at work?"

"Yeah, fine."

"No repercussions then?"

"No, Smithson's been great. He's had my corner all the way. I told you, he just thinks it's one big coincidence that Jamal was related to me. Well, I suppose it is really. If we hadn't have been to that place the night before, I might still have been involved in the police raid."

"Ah, well. It's a good job he's on your side, I suppose. Let's hope it stays that way, and that they never find out about the paedo."

"Don't worry, no one will find out about that, Rita. Me, you and Yansis are the only people who know; I haven't even told Paula."

"Maybe it's best that way, eh?"

"Definitely. It wasn't my finest hour so I'd rather we forget about it."

"Sure, I know you had your reasons."

Rita noticed that he didn't respond straightaway, and his previous comment seemed a bit sharp. Then, as though attempting to fill the awkward silence between them, he asked, "When do you go back?"

"Sunday."

"Bloody hell, that soon?"

"Yeah. Well, I didn't see any point waiting around now Daniel's a lot better, and I think it will do him good to get back."

"Do you need a lift to the airport?"

"No, Julie and Vinny are taking us, but thanks for offering."

"No probs. Will you have a chance to call round and say goodbye before you go?"

"Probably not. It's gonna be a mad rush with all the packing and everything. We've got to take Daniel for a check-up at the doctors tomorrow, just to make sure he's alright before the trip. Then, I'll be going to Mam and Dad's on Saturday afternoon to say my goodbyes. You could nip round there if you've time though, and I can say goodbye to all of you at the same time."

"I'll try, but I'm working a long shift. I'll do my best though."

"Oh, OK … well, I suppose this might be the last time I speak to you then. Don't forget you and Paula are welcome to come and stay in Greece any time. We'd love to have you."

"I might just take you up on that. Bye Rita, see you soon."

"Bye John."

As she cut the call she felt overwhelmed by emotion as well as a sense of guilt. It was as though there was a barrier between her and her brother; brought about by the trauma they'd shared.

Rita wished she had never got him involved. If John

hadn't been so immersed in what was happening to Daniel, then perhaps he wouldn't have harmed the paedophile. She knew that he would carry the death of Maurice James on his conscience for a long time.

Rita hoped that it hadn't affected their relationship. The conversation was definitely stilted in parts. Perhaps she was being oversensitive because of everything that had happened. He had offered her a lift to the airport when all was said and done.

John was her only remaining sibling and, under normal circumstances, she would have enjoyed the time she spent with him. It was her bad fortune that something so devastating should happen when she hadn't seen her brother for years, and she regretted that it had all gone so wrong.

Chapter 34

Sunday 30ᵗʰ June 1996

The day of their departure arrived. Rita, Yansis and Daniel were in the check-in queue at Manchester airport. Julie, Vinny and the children had joined them, refusing to leave until the last minute.

As they waited, the children became restless, and Yansis and Vinny were doing their best to occupy them by playing games of I Spy. The fact that he was going back to Greece hadn't yet fully registered with Daniel. Rita was sure that once the moment came when he had to say goodbye to Thomas and Emily, he wouldn't be very pleased.

Rita's mind wandered back to the previous day when she had said her final goodbyes to her parents. It was a difficult day. She had visited alone, still refusing to take Daniel to the Riverhill Estate. In fact, recent events made her more determined to keep him away. She was afraid that her parents' home would remind him too much of Raeni's and she didn't want that memory to resurface the day before they were to leave. Her mother's disappointment was evident when Rita walked in alone, and she felt bad.

That wasn't the only thing she felt bad about. Rita had toyed with the idea of saying goodbye to Raeni. Despite what she did in keeping Daniel, Rita felt an empathy towards her. But she dismissed the idea. There was no point in raking things up again; it was best to put it all behind her. As much as she was sorry for Raeni, she couldn't be held responsible for her situation.

The atmosphere at her parents' home had been awkward. Her father was his usual self, and her mother remained downcast throughout the visit. To make matters worse, John didn't show up. Not only did Rita feel disappointed, but she also felt despair that perhaps things would never be the same.

"Here we go," said Vinny, which caught Rita's attention. The two men were loading the cases onto the weighing platform while Julie was keeping the children out of the way.

"Oh, let me help," said Rita, taking Daniel's hand and leading him away from the counter.

When the last of the cases was loaded, Vinny said, "Right, we'll meet you at the entrance to Departures in a few minutes."

As Rita had anticipated, Daniel became agitated the moment Thomas and Emily were led away. His clinginess was still apparent.

"It's OK, Daniel," she reassured him. "We'll see them in a minute."

She waited until they checked in before explaining to Daniel that they were now going to say goodbye. Before he had a chance to get upset, she told him that it was something they must do before they could go back to his grandparents in Greece. The thought of seeing them calmed him down.

They had almost reached Julie, Vinny and the children when Rita heard somebody shout her name. She turned around to see her brother, John, and his wife, Paula, rushing towards them. She let Daniel run the last few metres to Julie and her family while she and Yansis waited for John and Paula to reach them.

"Thank God we got to you in time!" said John, pausing to catch his breath. "Sorry I couldn't make it yesterday. I didn't have a minute 'cos of work, but I wanted to come and see you off."

They shared hugs then went to join the rest of their party.

"We've brought Mam and Dad too," said John, pointing to their parents who were making their way across the airport terminal. "We thought it would be nice for us all to wave you off."

Rita met her parents halfway, giving them both a hug. Her mother was anxious to see Daniel, and they soon joined the others. They exchanged greetings, and Joan made a fuss of Daniel.

"Eeh, he doesn't look so bad considering, does he?" said Ged, referring to Daniel.

"Subtle as a brick, Dad, as always," laughed John.

"What?" asked Ged, nonplussed. "Eh, I'll tell you what, I was right all along about the lad. I told you our Irene didn't have him, didn't I, Joan?" he asked, while Joan gave him a mild poke in the ribs.

The rest of the adults laughed. Rita was overjoyed at them all coming to see her off, and even her father's bluntness didn't bother her. Their presence at the airport meant so much to her. They were all aware that this could be the last she saw of them for some time.

She was adamant that she wouldn't return to Manchester, and she doubted that her parents would visit Greece again despite her offer to put them up. Previous occasions hadn't exactly been a success.

They stood around for several minutes exchanging pleasantries until Yansis announced that it was time to go.

"I've just got one last bit of news before we leave you," said John. "We've booked the honeymoon."

"Oh, that's great," said Rita. "Where are you going?"

"Greece. On the 27th July. For two weeks. That's if the offer's still open."

Rita stared back at him, open-mouthed.

"To stay with you and Yansis, I mean."

Rita was delighted, "Yeah, course it is!" she said, giving them both another hug.

She would be seeing her brother and his wife in a few weeks' time! And, even better, was the knowledge that their relationship had survived all they had been through. In fact, rather than driving a wedge between them, it had probably brought them closer.

To her consternation, she could feel tears of joy pricking her eyes. "Yeah that's great," she said, bending to straighten Daniel's trousers. It was a subterfuge to hide her tears, but she underestimated her son's perception.

"Why are you crying, Mummy?" he asked, trouncing his grandfather for lack of subtlety.

"Give over, Daniel. Mummy isn't crying; Mummy never cries."

THE END

Author Note

If you enjoyed 'Danger by Association' perhaps you would consider leaving a review on Amazon using the direct link: www.amazon.co.uk/dp/B01FE2A2BU for readers in the UK or www.amazon.com/dp/B01FE2A2BU for readers in the US. Independent authors such as myself value reader reviews, and we rely on them to spread the word about our work.

I am also inviting readers to subscribe to my mailing list by following the link: http://eepurl.com/CP6YP. This will enable you to be among the first to find out about forthcoming publications, and receive a FREE copy of my short story book 'Crime, Conflict & Consequences'. I use my mailing list solely to notify readers about my books and will never share your details with any third parties.

***

About the Author

Heather Burnside started her writing career seventeen years ago when she began to work as a freelance writer while studying towards her writing diploma. During that time she had many articles published in well-known UK magazines. As part of her studies Heather began work on her debut novel, 'Slur', and wrote several short stories. She has since written outlines for a number of other novels.

Despite interest from a couple of literary agents, Heather didn't quite succeed in finding a mainstream publisher for 'Slur'. Disheartened, she eventually put it to one side while she focused on developing her writing services business, but was determined to return to it one day.

Through her writing services business, Heather has ghost-written many non-fiction books on behalf of clients covering a broad range of topics. However, she now prefers to concentrate on fiction writing.

'Danger by Association' is the third book in 'The Riverhill Trilogy'. The first two books in the trilogy, entitled 'Slur' and 'A Gangster's Grip', are available from Amazon. Heather has also published a collection of short stories which is available for download on Amazon Kindle. You can find all of Heather's books on Amazon by checking out her Amazon author page at: http://Author.to/HBurnside.

Heather publishes regular updates about her writing on her blog at: www.heatherburnside.com. You can also connect with her on Twitter at: @heatherbwriter or on Facebook at: www.facebook.com/DMPublisher.

***

Acknowledgements

I would like to thank everybody who has given me help and support during the writing of this book. This includes the community of authors and avid readers who are always on hand to answer questions and point me in the right direction.

During the research stage of this book I utilised a number of handy resources. As well as referring to Internet sites on the topics of prisoner rehabilitation, the probation service, programmes for sex offenders, gang warfare, weather reports, the Iraq war and general points of law, I also consulted books. To get a feel for what it was like during the Allied Forces mission in Iraq during 1991, I found the following books helpful: 'The One that Got Away' by Chris Ryan, and 'Victor Two: Inside Iraq: the Crucial SAS Mission' by Peter Crossland. The Police History Society was also very helpful in answering my questions relating to policing in 1996 so I would like to extend my thanks to them.

Thanks also go to my excellent team of beta readers who have given valuable feedback to help me improve the book. They are the lovely Guy Portman, Sophia Carleton, Kath Middleton, Bill Kupersmith, Emma Dellow and Rita Ackerman.

Big thanks also to the very talented Chris Howard for once again designing a top-notch book cover. Chris is great to work with. He can translate your initial ideas into wonderful finished products, but is also willing to give input if he has other suggestions. You can contact Chris at: blondesign@gmail.com.

I would like to thank my friends for all their support, not only with this book but ever since I started my career as a published author. Last but not least, I would like to thank my wonderful family for all the support they have given me in bringing this book to market.

***

Disclaimer

All of the characters in 'Danger by Association' are fictitious. They are products of the author's imagination and are not intended to bear any resemblance whatsoever to real people. Likewise, the character's names have been invented by the author, and any similarity to the names of real people is purely coincidental.

***

You might like to read an excerpt from Heather's next novel, 'Bad Brother and I', which is due for publication in early 2017.

Bad Brother and I

As soon as Adele walked into the back garden she was horrified by the sight that met her. Among the overgrown bushes and weed-filled borders was an assortment of cracked and mossy flagstones that acted as a path. There, her brother, Peter, stood facing her. He was wielding a large twig which he had stripped bare. For him it now represented a whip; flexible enough to slash rapidly through the air, yet strong enough to inflict damage.

He chuckled with glee as he repeatedly thrashed his whip onto the paving slabs in front of him. His target was several squirming caterpillars of differing sizes and various shades of green and brown, which he had lined up. Adele could see their tiny bodies writhing as savage blows from the handmade whip assailed them, causing their oozing entrails to spill out onto the path.

"Stop it!" she shouted.

Peter paused briefly to reply, "Don't be daft. They're only insects."

"I don't care. It's cruel and disgusting," Adele countered, becoming agitated.

"You're stupid, you are. I'm not doing any harm. Go and mither someone else, Miss Goody-goody."

"At least I'm not like you!"

"What do you mean?"

Adele could sense his change in tone, but, despite her unease, she refused to give way. "You're always up to no good, you are. You're gonna get in trouble again if you don't

1

watch it."

"Oh shut up, you cry baby! Go and play with your dolls."

Ignoring her pleas, Peter continued to mete out his vicious punishment.

Adele felt her stomach lurch at the sickening sight and cried out to him, "Peter, stop it; it's horrible!"

Unfortunately, her cries soon reached the ears of their father who sped through the back door, pushing her aside. She noticed that he was still in his shabby vest, and knew that he hadn't been out of bed long, even though it was midday. She instinctively sensed that he wouldn't take kindly to having his Sunday disturbed.

"What the bleedin' hell's going on here?" he demanded.

Peter dropped the whip and looked up guiltily at his father. His jaw hung loose but he failed to utter any words of defence. Their father didn't need a reply, however, as his eyes took in the revolting sight. In one stride he was on Peter grabbing at his shirt collar, and thrusting upwards until his feet left the ground.

"You dirty little get!" he yelled. "Look at the bleedin' state of that path."

He released his hold, allowing Peter to drop shakily to the ground. Then, prodding his forefinger into Peter's face, he ordered, "Get it cleaned up … NOW!"

Peter hung his head in shame and approached the house in search of something with which to clean up the mess.

"Where the bleedin' hell do you think you're going?" roared his father. "I told you to clean them up."

"I'm going for some newspaper to wipe them up with," Peter replied.

"No you're bleedin' not! You weren't bothered about newspaper when you put the bleedin' things there, so why bother now? You can get them shifted with yer hands. And I want every bit cleared up including that slimy shit that's come out of 'em. That'll teach you, you dirty little swine!"

He turned and pushed Adele aside again as he trundled back indoors. Just before stepping into the house, he turned his head back and added, "And you can get your bleedin' hands washed when you've finished as well."

For a few moments Adele stood transfixed. She was too numbed by the incident to react straightaway.

"What you looking at, you bitch?" muttered Peter. "It's all your fault! If you hadn't started carrying on, he wouldn't have known."

As he murmured these few words, he made a show of wiping up the slimy mess with his fingers.

Adele couldn't take any more. She ran into the house retching, and headed straight for her bedroom where she threw herself onto the bed. But the tears didn't come. At eleven years of age, she'd suppressed her tears so often that it had become an automatic defence mechanism that helped her get through these frequent occurrences.

Adele felt bad. She shouldn't have carried on so much at Peter. It was bound to annoy her father, especially on a Sunday. He was always in a mood on a Sunday. In fact, he was always in a mood any day, but Sundays were particularly bad.

It was only lately, as she was growing up, that Adele realised why; it was because of the skinful he had had on a Saturday night. All he wanted to do on Sundays was sleep it off. Then he would sit and pore through the papers whilst their mother, Shirley, made a pretence of cleaning the house, and cooked the traditional Sunday dinner in an effort to please him.

This was usually the first attempt at cleaning that Shirley had made all week. She spent most of her days gossiping with the neighbours, sleeping or watching TV. Her evenings were spent in a similar fashion, except for the few nights a week in which she tore herself away from the street to go and play bingo.

After consoling herself, Adele lifted herself up off the bed and drifted towards the window. She avoided the sight of Peter, but looked out instead at the other houses, watching people go about their business. Allowing her mind to drift, she contemplated, for the umpteenth time, her miserable existence.

Lately she was realising that although this way of life was commonplace within these four walls, there was a different world out there. Talking to her friends had made her understand that her circumstances weren't the norm, and that other parents were different from her own. Other children went out with their families to the cinema or country parks. They had holidays at the seaside and expensive presents for their birthdays.

The only advantage she had over other children was her freedom. Her father was hardly ever home, so that gave her and Peter a chance to roam the streets and do whatever they pleased as long as news of their mischief didn't get back to him. Their mother was indifferent, and scarcely showed any interest in where they were going or what time they would be back.

Sometimes Adele would wander to the local playground, which contained an assortment of battered apparatus on an unkempt patch of ground. There she would climb to the top of the climbing frame and escape from her world by pretending she was a princess standing inside a tall tower and surveying her land. The people there all worked for her, and it was their job to do as she ordered. She was the head of the kingdom and everybody had to bow to her and make her happy.

She consoled herself by imagining that one day the dream could almost become a reality. When she was old enough she would get a good job and a rich husband, and she would escape from her domineering father and slovenly mother. She would have a beautiful home and children who would never want for anything. It was this dream that kept her going.

Just then Adele was jolted back to reality by the sound of raised voices downstairs.

"Don't go Tommy, I was gonna do you a nice dinner later," pleaded her mother.

"Bugger off, I'm going for a pint. There's nowt to stay in this bloody pigsty for. I'm sick of you, you lazy cow, and those two scruffy little gets!"

This was followed by a loud slamming of the front door and Shirley muttering something to herself. Adele couldn't quite hear her mother's words, but she surmised that she wasn't happy with her father's exit.

Adele had had enough of home for one day. She decided that she would go outside for a while, maybe call for one of her friends. Perhaps she would see if Peter wanted to go out, if he had calmed down by now. She was heading downstairs when she heard the sound of the door knocker. Fearing that her father was returning, she backtracked to the top of the stairs. It was only after her mother had answered the door that Adele realised it was her grandma, Betty.

She entered loudly, and, appearing as bumptious as ever, commented, "I've just passed His Lordship in the street. He's got a right face on him, as usual. It took him all his time to say hello. What the bleedin' hell's up with him this time?"

Shirley said nothing, but shook her head from side to side as she led her mother into the living room. Adele would normally have fled down the stairs to greet her grandma, who she thought the world of. Although loud and opinionated, Betty had a kind heart and was full of good intentions. But the look of resignation on her mother's face, and the tired way she dragged her feet, stopped Adele from following them.

She had guessed that they were about to have one of their conversations. Overcome by curiosity, she crept down the stairs so she could overhear them.

"Jesus, Shirley love, what the bloody hell's happened to this place? It looks like a bomb's hit it, and it smells bloody awful! It's worse than last time. I thought you were going to try and keep on top of things!"

"Oh don't start, Mam. Don't you think I'm sick of it? It's not me that makes it a tip you know, and what's the use of tidying it anyway when they only mess it up again?"

"I'm worried about you, love. Every time I come you've let yourself go more. You're just not happy, are you? Has he been at you again?"

"Not really. It's Peter he's pissed off with, because he made a mess on the garden path, squashing some caterpillars or summat. I wish he'd leave him alone; he's not a bad lad really."

"I don't know, I worry about our Peter, always up to mischief and getting into fights. I've told you, he takes after his side of the family."

Their conversation then became much quieter, and Adele had to strain to hear them. Without getting too close, and risking being caught out, she managed to catch snippets of her grandma's words.

"Bad lot … told you before … bad blood … mad … great uncle … always fighting … ended up in an asylum."

A few moments of silence followed until Shirley said, "I don't know what I'm gonna do, Mam. I've no idea what our Peter will turn out like. I'm just glad our Adele's all right."

"Aye, she's a good girl," replied Betty whose voice had returned to its normal level. "Keep encouraging her to do well at school so she can bugger off to university or summat. She'll be bloody better off out of it."

Betty's voice then adopted a sympathetic tone. "I do worry about you, Shirley love. You don't seem to care anymore. Did you go to the doctors like I told you to?"

"Yeah, he's given me these for the daytime on top of the ones I take at night."

"Let's have a look," said Betty who then tried to read the words on the bottle of pills. "Dia ... ze ... pam. What are they supposed to do?"

Betty didn't realise that Diazepam was the clinical name for Valium.

"I don't know," said Shirley. "But I feel more knackered than ever. I've not got the energy I was born with, honestly Mam."

"Well, I don't know what the bloody hell to make of it all. I wish to God you'd never married him in the first place. I tried to warn you, but you wouldn't be told. I'd take you and the kids round to my house, but I've just not got the room."

"I know that, Mam. I've just got to put up with it, haven't I? Besides, I love Tommy. I just wish he wasn't so angry all the time."

Betty looked exasperated, but didn't continue. It was a topic which she had already covered many times before, so she moved onto something else. When Adele had grown tired of hearing about what Betty's neighbours were up to, she returned to her bedroom. There she mulled over the conversation in her young mind.

She knew her grandmother had been referring to her father, Tommy, and his family. She was used to her grandma Betty calling them, but she had never heard her mention the word 'mad' before. Maybe it was just a figure of speech, meaning they had bad tempers. She wondered about the word asylum. It wasn't one she was familiar with, but she decided to check it in her dictionary.

Adele took her dictionary off the row of books on the shelf. She opened it up, and scanned the words under the letter 'a' to see if asylum was listed. She found two meanings; the first of them referred to a place of refuge but the second related to a mental institution. She wondered which of these her grandma could have been talking about but she daren't ask. Something in her subconscious linked the second definition to her grandma's use of the word 'mad'. But she wasn't sure. It was all so confusing, and too much for a girl of eleven to interpret.

She was curious about the tablets her mother was taking as well; something called Diazepam, her grandma had said. Adele flicked over the pages of her dictionary again, checking whether Diazepam was listed, but she couldn't find anything.

As she looked through the dictionary, her thoughts drifted away from the misery of her home situation. Adele began to play a game she had devised to entertain herself. It involved opening the dictionary at random, and pointing to a word with her eyes shut. When she opened her eyes, she had to guess what the word meant without reading the definition first. This was one of the many uses she found from her beloved dictionary, which she had chosen when she won a book prize at school.

When she grew tired of looking through the dictionary, she selected an Enid Blyton book she had borrowed from the library, and immersed herself in the adventures of the Famous Five. It was her guilty pleasure. Adele's teacher was trying to encourage her to read more challenging books because of her advanced reading age, but Adele enjoyed the escapism that the Famous Five books provided. Within minutes Enid Blyton had successfully diverted Adele's attention from all the troubles of the day.

***

Printed in Great Britain
by Amazon